BREAKAWAY

BREAKAWAY

Paul Yee

A Groundwood Book
Douglas & McIntyre
Toronto/Vancouver/Buffalo

Groundwood Books/Douglas & McIntyre
585 Bloor Street West
Toronto, Ontario M6G 1K5

Distributed in the U.S.A. by Publishers Group West
4065 Hollis Street
Emeryville, CA 94608

The publisher gratefully acknowledges the assistance of the
Canada Council and the Ontario Arts Council.

Canadian Cataloguing in Publication Data

Yee, Paul
Breakaway

ISBN 0-88899-201-7

I. Title.

PS8597.E3B7 1994   jC813'.54   C93-095543-9
PZ7.Y44Br 1994

Cover illustration by Laurie McGaw
Design by Michael Solomon
Printed and bound in Canada

Dedicated to Vancouver's Chinese Students Soccer Club, winners of the Iroquois Cup (1926), the Wednesday League Cup (1931), the B.C. Mainland Cup (1934) and the Spalding Cup (1937).

ONE

THE Model T lurched and shuddered to a stop. Kwok-Ken Wong could hear the rain drumming steadily onto the canvas roof above and into the big tin tubs on the truck's open deck. Water dripped dark from the fire-escape ladder hanging on the nearby building and washed over the cobblestones down towards the sewer. The storm had driven the scavenging cats indoors and capped the dank smells of garbage.

Kwok scanned the alley with anxious eyes. The laneway stood empty. He breathed with relief. Still, he sank lower into the hard, well-worn seat. Once, two teenage girls had come chasing through, laughing and giggling. They had stopped when they saw Kwok working. He had been so ashamed he wouldn't look at them.

Ba got out of the truck and pounded at the back door of the Chung King Restaurant with both fists. But the wood was thick and heavy and the rain deadened his shouts for Head Cook.

He turned to Kwok and said sharply, "Go front and have them open up." Then he went to untie the tubs. Years ago Ba had cut away the back of the Model T and fitted a plank floor there. The job had taken him a week, but when he was finished, he had grinned proudly for days. Pretty soon all the other Chinese farmers were doing the same thing, buying old cars and remaking them into handy farm trucks.

When Kwok did not stir, his father shook his head. Without wasting another second, he strode down the alleyway, hunching his head and shoulders against the driving rain. Then he heard the truck door slam and the muffled sound of his son's footsteps.

Kwok followed quickly, his head down as he watched his boot-tips darken from the rain. The workboots were battered and loose, abandoned in the Wongs' barn by some transient farmhand. If only someone would leave behind some nice downtown clothes, Kwok often thought. Some nice baggy pants that hung loose and full like those worn by the fellows at school who knew the latest fashions. Maybe a hotshot Chinatown gambler who had been caught cheating would be fleeing Vancouver for the United States border. He'd pass by the farm, take shelter and leave his clothes to disguise himself in Kwok's grimy overalls and baggy sweater.

Kwok rounded the corner, and a rickety car twisted by on narrow tires. Not too many automobiles could be seen. When it rained, drivers stayed indoors, unless they drove one of the fancy new models with glass windows all around and windshield wipers up front.

Still, the main street was crowded with people. Umbrellas slick with spring rain passed Kwok on both sides. They tilted up, and curious eyes observed him momentarily. Brick buildings three storeys high lined the street; dark windows stood in solemn rows behind wrought-iron balconies. The men of Chinatown lived up there in tiny grimy rooms.

Kwok ducked under the storefront awnings and hurried to catch up to his father.

I hate coming here, he thought. Chinatown people look at us and think the Wongs are low-life. We track farm mud wherever we go. People hold their noses when we come close. They sweep up as soon as we've passed. We beggars do anything to feed our pigs for cheap.

Shoppers clustered around sodden bins of green vegetables glistening in the rain. Some children tugging at their mother shrank back when they saw Kwok's grim expression.

At the Chung King Restaurant he turned in and bumped into Ba, who stood waiting. Kwok looked away and caught his own reflection in a dark pane of glass. His face was square and solid, and the dark eyes under the thick black eyebrows stared back boldly. But it was the ruddy red colouring of his cheeks that made him look twelve years old forever.

Inside, the restaurant was half empty, with men scattered at tables and booths on all sides. Dirty curtains of tobacco smoke drifted aimlessly in greyish wisps. The menu strips lining the walls curled from age and neglect.

It used to be that the place throbbed with noisy crowds. Men would eat, argue, play gambling games over lengthy meals and endless drinks, and laugh as loud as they pleased. Today, the waiters turned away abruptly as soon as they recognized Ba.

Kwok followed his father towards the back, hearing wooden chairs creak and bodies shift. The same thing happened every time they walked in: the shiny noses of twenty uneasy men sniffed them like hunting dogs. Some men seemed to spend all their days here, now that jobs were scarce. This was their only home.

Ba kept his eyes fixed ahead. No one ever called out to them or pulled them over to sit and share some food or conversation. Years ago, when Ba discovered how he had been cheated in the gambling halls, he lost his temper and publicly denounced all these men who dawdled their days away like house cats. No one had ever forgotten.

We don't live here in Chinatown, so they think we're oddballs, Kwok thought. They think we smell like pigs. Well, when I go to university I'll leave town and never see this place again. He ploughed through the swinging doors to the kitchen with an angry shove.

"Hey, you! Kwok-ah!" A hearty voice boomed out of the steam and crackling that sputtered from a row of stovetop woks. It was Head Cook. A smudged brown apron covered his ample belly, and his grey hair bristled short and thick like an army private's. He brandished thick cooking chopsticks, which he suddenly flicked. A piece of sizzling meat came flying.

Kwok caught it and yelped. "Ouch! Hot!"

Head Cook grinned. "No heat, no eat."

Kwok tossed the steaming morsel from palm to palm. Then he bit in, and the hot spicy juices danced through his mouth. Ba was at the sink, gulping water from a cracked enamel mug.

Head Cook lifted the lids of the woks, and steam enveloped him instantly. Briskly he scooped the hot food onto plates and jangled the bell calling the waiters. When he turned around, the Wongs stood waiting.

Ba spoke gruffly. "Anything under the sink?"

Head Cook nodded and Ba tramped by. Whoever did dish duty emptied the food left from the tables into a lard pail under the sink. Once full, it went downstairs to await pick-up by Ba and Kwok and transformation into a second life as feed for the pigs they raised on their farm. Nothing was wasted in 1932 Chinatown, especially since the Depression had descended, devouring jobs and futures everywhere.

Head Cook swung around to Kwok, his grin baring a mouthful of gold-capped teeth. "They're playing today, you know that?"

"Of course," Kwok replied. "I saw the newspaper. Against Alumni. The last time the Chinese played them, we lost. Think we'll lose again?"

"We'd better not." Head Cook scowled. "I need my winnings." Then he brightened. "That last game, it was bad luck. But the horoscope predicts today is my lucky day."

Along with most of Chinatown, Head Cook loyally attended every game of the Chinese Soccer Team. He gambled heavily on them, too, like most men.

Kwok leaned forward eagerly. Head Cook was the only one in Chinatown who talked soccer with him. "How could they have lost?" Kwok asked. "Alumni is the worst team in the league. They're last in the standings."

His friend nodded emphatically. "I remember they were so bad at one game that they scored for us."

Kwok's eyes lit up. "Really?"

The old man grinned at the memory. "Our side had pushed them in front of their goal all day long. Most of the game, it had been played there. The Alumni men were like newly hatched chicks chasing a mother hen all over the field. A few steps here, a few steps there. Round and round they spun."

Kwok picked up a piece of barbecued meat and waved it at the cook, who nodded. He popped the morsel into his mouth and chewed noisily as Head Cook continued his story. "Our side was running circles around them. The other side didn't know front from back. And then one fellow turned and punted the ball into his own net."

Kwok shook his head. "No one could be that stupid," he said. "I don't believe it."

Head Cook pretended to be insulted. "You don't believe it, you don't have to stand here and talk to me."

"I've played hundreds of games," Kwok insisted. "It could never happen."

"What do schoolboys know?" Head Cook raised an eyebrow in a mock salute.

Kwok retorted, "I'm good enough to play on the inter-school team."

"That's not real soccer," Head Cook said, grinning.

Ba dragged the lard pail to the head of the stairs and glared at Kwok. "Start work," he ordered.

Reluctantly, Kwok broke away from Head Cook.

"The game starts in half an hour," Head Cook called out. "Want to come?"

Kwok looked up quickly, glad that Head Cook had issued the invitation aloud so that his father could not avoid hearing. He held his breath. If he looked too eager to go, then for sure Ba would say no. But Kwok could not cap the pleading that shone through his eyes.

Ba shook his head firmly. "There's plenty of work at home. You think heaven will send fairies down to do your chores?"

"But I'll get everything done," Kwok promised.

Ba moved towards the door. He did not like his authority challenged in public. "Your mother, she wants you to look at your books. You and those examinations, fah!"

"It's the start of the—" Kwok faltered, groping for the Chinese words for tournament, championship and trophy. He didn't know them; they weren't part of everyday family conversation. Lamely he muttered, "They're playing to see who's the best team in town."

"Hey, Ah-Hoi, your son plays soccer," exclaimed Head Cook. "Let him come."

Ba turned and tugged at the heavy pail. "Waste of time. Come on."

Frustrated, Kwok sucked in a breath noisily. He had not seen a single game this season. School-work, homework, farmwork, and now this pig slop work. It wasn't fair. He was eighteen years old and still being ordered around by his father.

The swinging doors opened again, and Kwok saw Ba's face tighten. A high-pitched voice called out, "Ah-Hoi, there you are."

Taro Head swung a toothpick from one side of his mouth to the other and fussed at the sleeve of his suit. On one hand flashed a jade ring framed in gold. Jauntily he tilted his snap brim hat back and licked his greasy lips. "Trying to avoid me?"

Ba forced a meek smile to his face as Kwok edged towards the back. Head Cook turned to his cooking, crooning an opera melody. Taro Head was one of Chinatown's rare new millionaires. He used to be one of the many "broken-legs" — men who gambled and drank their days and nights away in the game halls and restaurants of Chinatown.

Ba swallowed hard and said tersely, "Mr. Woo, I know I'm late, but I'll make payment next month. For certain."

Kwok went down the stairs to the basement. Two years ago, Taro Head had won big in the gambling pool. Now he was lending money to the farmers like an upstart new bank.

The storeroom below was dim and narrow, lit only from the distant back door. But Kwok's nose pulled him directly to two heavy drums of pig slop. The sweaty slush of rice, meat, sauce and soups had been decaying for days from the heat of the ovens above. Kwok had never gotten used to the sour stink of the slop. He held his breath and swung one container up the stairs as fast as he could go.

Outside, Ba waited for him behind the truck. The visor on his cap was wilting from the rain. Kwok heard him muttering angrily about Taro Head. Together they reached for the drum. Heaving it to their shoulders, they tilted it over a tin tub.

"Not so fast," warned Ba. Precious brown ooze splattered onto the truck deck.

Kwok averted his eyes. Skinflint Ba had to save every scrap.

"I said not so fast." His father's voice grated into a threat.

Kwok twisted viciously, forcing his side of the heavy container down. The slop spattered out thickly.

Suddenly Ba lost his grip. The drum flipped sideways and slop shot over Kwok. He fell back and dropped everything, howling in disgust and fury. Slop covered him from head to toe. Choking and spitting, he tried to clear the acrid taste of cigarette ash and rancid oil from his mouth.

"Told you to slow down," Ba muttered. "Now look at you."

"Look at me? Look at you!" Kwok danced around, stomping his feet, wiping his face, trying to shake and brush himself clean. He wanted to grab his father's neck and ram him into the cobblestones. You push me around like a mutt dog and scream at me in front of other people. You throw this slop over me and make it all my fault.

"Sweep it up fast," Ba ordered. He threw a shovel and broom stub over.

Kwok let them clatter to the ground. His hands clawed at the gobs of oily food sticking to him. Grains of rice here, a chicken bone there, a bok-choy leaf on his shoulder. Kwok felt contaminated, spat upon by a hundred dripping mouths. He wet his hands in puddle water and scrubbed at his face.

Ba emerged from the basement weighed down by the other drum and called out wearily, "Sweep it up. Hurry."

Kwok sniffed his sweater and winced. Now he did smell like the pigs at home. He grabbed the broom and banged it around his legs, trying to scrape the stench off. He saw the rain tug and pull at the slop. In another few minutes, the storm would wash all the cobblestones clean.

Ba came over and yanked the broom from Kwok. With several swift strokes, he swept brown slop and rain water onto the shovel and tossed it into the tub.

"Get in." He tied the tubs down securely.

Kwok did not move. He stood like a statue, legs spread wide, face to the heavens and eyes shut. He wanted to stand there until the rain washed him clean of all slop and stink. I hope I get soaked to the skin and catch pneumonia and die, he thought. If only the rain could bleach away the black of this hair and make me someone else.

Ba cranked the engine and the Model T rattled to life. Kwok waited as long as he dared before scrambling aboard. He banged the gate shut and turned away from his father, hurling silent curses at him. Breathing loudly through his teeth, he tried to keep the smell out of his nose.

The truck rolled out of the alley and onto the main street of Chinatown. The Dai Wah, another restaurant that used to offer them pig slop, had newspapers plastered over its windows to announce its bankruptcy. The butcher shop next door was now the office for raising funds against the Japanese invasion of China. Last fall, Japan had seized control of the northern province of Manchuria. Since the beginning of the year, the Chinese army had been fighting Japanese troops in the city of Shanghai.

A group of men strolled out of the Chung King, adjusted their hats and caps, and started running. Probably going to the soccer game, Kwok thought. Nothing could stop the people of Chinatown from going out, even in the rain, to watch their team.

It had been a surprise and an honour when the Chinese team entered the district men's league two years ago. They were the first Asians to play in the league, against powerful teams from the police, the university and the Scottish community. Big companies sponsored the teams, and the Chinatown team was backed by the Gim Lee Yuen Company, a long-established firm on Pender Street. The games always drew big crowds because they were free and situated at nearby downtown pitches. Last year the Chinese team had advanced all the way to the Northwest Trophy semi-finals before being beaten. In these difficult times, celebrations were rare in Chinatown.

Grinding loudly, the truck rolled south onto Main Street and sped up. Here the Chinese monopoly on storefronts dissolved as the Japanese barber, the Jewish tailor, the pawnshops, the Italian importer and the tobacco confectioneries took up places. To the south, the dark clouds were lifting.

"Better check the dykes as soon as we get home," Ba said. "The river is running high. The mountain snow up-country is melting fast this year."

A streetcar clanged and swooshed by on the shiny steel tracks imbedded in the road. Behind it ambled a vegetable pedlar and his horse-drawn cart. The animal's skin sagged dull and dirty over jutting bones. Going door to door on a day like this to sell greens and fruits to lazy housewives was killing this horse. Time to turn the animal into fertilizer, Kwok thought. Time to join the automobile age.

When had he last seen some Chinatown soccer? Kwok tried to remember. Probably last fall, after harvest. At the Cambie Street Grounds. He remembered squeezing through the crowd, the ache of his shoulders evaporating like mist skimming off the river early in the morning. The players on the field in their royal blue jerseys were a few years older than him but few were as big. They called out to each other in the Toisan dialect even though they all spoke fluent English.

"Watch out behind!"

"In the centre!"

The Chinese they shouted was loud and deliberate, taunting their opponents with instructions and tips that only they could understand.

Kwok could never call out in Chinese in public. He could never see himself playing here, no matter how much he loved soccer. He didn't belong in Chinatown. He didn't have any friends here. Ba had kept his family far away from Chinatown after he quit drinking and gambling.

Kwok had followed the soccer intently, looking for tips to use in his own game. The Chinese used one simple strategy: kick and run. They ran faster, being smaller in build, so they sent the ball cannoning down the field and charged after it like racehounds.

The truck hurtled through the intersection with a jolt. Ba wanted to beat the red light to save gas and avoid pressing the brakes to reduce their wear and tear. Besides, the truck needed a good start to run up the hill.

Then Kwok gasped. From the right side, a sportster charged towards them at full speed. The driver was looking out the other side window.

"The horn!" Kwok shouted, throwing his arms up over his face.

Ba yanked the wheel hard right. The truck tilted and careened dizzily onto the sidewalk. A crash followed, glass shattered, and Kwok's head thumped into the roof-beam. Ba raced out. Kwok blinked hard to clear the thud from his head and followed. Still shuddering, the truck teetered half on the road and half on the sidewalk. Its right front had dug into the brick wall of a store, cracking the headlamp.

The sportster had pulled over to the other side and Ba shouted at the driver to get out. Quickly, Kwok pushed his way through the gathering crowd.

Ba had pulled the offending driver out by his jacket lapels and was shaking him vigorously. Then Kwok recognized the face, and dismay exploded inside him. "Phil?"

"Kwok!" A smile of relief relaxed the face of the young man Ba had seized. "You know this fellow?"

Kwok grabbed his father's arm and hissed, "Ba, let him go."

"You know him?" Ba sounded surprised.

Kwok nodded quickly. "He's in my class."

Ba thrust him away and swore under his breath. "Almost killed us."

Phil was adjusting his cap and straightening his jacket when Ba grabbed his arm. "You hit my truck. You pay me!"

The young man shook him loose. "I didn't even touch you," he retorted. His finger poked Ba on the chest. "You were the one who hit the wall."

"You go through red light," Ba persisted.

"You went through the amber," Phil said evenly, crossing his arms over his chest.

"I got lots time."

Kwok pulled urgently at his father. "Ba, let's go," he pleaded.

Ba flung Kwok's arm off. "You pay me," he said to Phil.

Phil shook his head and thrust out his jaw. "I don't owe you a penny."

"You make the accident, you pay me." Ba reached for Phil again, but the young man ducked like a boxer.

"Get out, Chinaman."

The words spat out from behind. Ba and Kwok spun around, but the circle of white faces stared back blankly. They were workers heading home from the sawmills, with lunchbuckets, heavy boots, caps coated with sawdust and oil. They were young secretaries and clerks with hats, glossy purses and long raincoats. No one claimed the words.

A muscle in Ba's cheek twitched. With a snort of disgust, he stalked off to his truck. Kwok breathed with relief and followed quickly.

Ba had climbed aboard the truck when Kwok spun around and sprinted back. Phil had just swung into his car and was sorting the overturned clutter of books beside him. Kwok stood by the running board and cleared his throat noisily. Phil looked up.

"Sorry about all this," Kwok muttered.

Phil shrugged. "Does your father always scream and push like that?"

"Yeah, no ... well, he loses his temper some-times ..."

"He sure does."

Kwok swallowed hard. "It wasn't your fault. The accident, that is."

"Tell your father that."

Kwok stuck his hands into his pockets and attempted a smile. "So, where are you going?"

"Ferry terminal." Phil reached for the gearshift. "I'm heading over to the Island."

"Oh. Well, have a good trip."

Kwok watched the car swing away. Phil was cap-tain of the school soccer team. He and Kwok were both forwards. Outstanding forwards, Kwok liked to think, on an outstanding team. Kwok used to watch Phil out of the sides of his eyes, hoping to catch a friendly grin. In the lunchroom, he used to wait for Phil to beckon to him. But Phil always had his own buddies around him and, during the past year, a cluster of girls sporting lipstick and grown-up sheer stockings had become part of his noisy, happy circle.

Ba sat in the truck, listening to the engine sput-ter and fade, sputter and fade. As soon as Kwok climbed in, the damp stench of the pig-slop hit him like a sodden blanket. Holy cats, he thought, sniff-ing at his sleeve, Phil must think our whole farm smells like this. He glared at Ba. Thanks to this old fool.

The truck backed up, then swung around into the traffic. It limped up the hill.

Finally Ba spoke. "That boy, does his family have money?"

"No!"

"If they don't have money, then why does he have such a nice car?"

Kwok looked out at the storefronts whizzing by and refused to answer.

Ba started again. "A boy like that, you don't need him for a friend."

Kwok seethed with silent anger. Friends? Yeah, I have plenty of friends. People are lining up and down the school hallway to spend time with me. Don't you know? I'm the only Chinese in the school.

TWO

K WOK and his father rode in silence for the remainder of the trip home. The Model T chugged steadily out from the city centre, passing through the elegant tree-lined avenues and the wooded outskirts of town before heading down to the river. From a distance, it loomed like sheet metal, steely and grey. On both sides of the water, reaching east and west as far as the eye could see, lay the farms of the Chinese market gardeners. The delta soil was lush and dark, cultivated in long rows that ran down to the bulky dykes keeping the river at bay.

The slop stink festered and simmered in Kwok's nose. As soon as I get home, he thought, I'm going to dump these clothes into a tub to soak and put on something clean. Then I'm staying inside. Let Ba check the dykes. Let him sweep the pigsty and weed his precious asparagus field.

The truck wheezed to an uncertain stop in the clearing and Kwok ran towards the house. A figure crouching on the porch unfolded suddenly and called out.

Lee Bing was their neighbour from down the road. A snap of irritation slowed Kwok. Every tool in the Wongs' barn had already been lent to Lee Bing at least three times over. He had also begged seed and fertilizer and seedlings from Ba. And crates and sacks and string, too. Ba never refused because Lee Bing had years enough to be his father. Unfortunately, the old man seemed to be shadowed by a cloud of bad luck season after season. When he planted carrots, weevils infested them. When he planted potatoes, the leaves turned purple, then brown. When he planted cabbages, worms burrowed into the heads. Ma always sent over leftover food, and even Kwok often felt sorry for him.

A slight, thin man, Lee Bing's gaunt face had been stretched by too much sun and wind. Today his eyes bulged frantically.

"My sow is dying!" he cried. He looked as if he had been weeping. "Two piglets came out dead. Black and hard as rocks."

Kwok sighed, and then he was running down the path that snaked through the bushes. Lee Bing had purchased the sow three months before, with the last of his borrowings from Taro Head. The old farmer had never raised pigs before, but had heard that piglets would fetch a good price. When Ba learned about the deal, he shook his head. He knew that if Lee Bing lost this sow and the piglets, the old farmer would be utterly ruined. Never would he repay Taro Head. Never would he return to China to spend his last days with his wife.

Lee Bing had neither a barn nor a proper pen for his pigs. Instead, posts and wooden boards covered with sheets of corrugated tin formed a rough enclosure. When Kwok crept in, he had to squint to see through the dark. He sucked in his breath at the dank smell of mould and rot. There was no straw to be seen anywhere, and the ground oozed with mud and manure. He brushed away the flies buzzing at his face.

The sow lay on its side, panting heavily in uneven snorts, grating its teeth painfully. Its long sagging stomach heaved and shuddered.

"Look at the legs," muttered Lee Bing, squatting behind Kwok. "Jerk this way, jerk that way. It's going to die for sure."

Kwok ran his hand gently over the sow's belly. "How long since the first ones came out?"

Lee Bing waggled his head. "Half an hour. I waited and waited, but no more came. They said there should be about eight or nine. So I ran over to you. Is it going to die?"

Kwok looked at the pig and swallowed hard. He pulled off his sodden jacket. He had seen this before and there was only one thing to do. "Do you have some clean rags or blankets?"

Rolling his sleeves up past his elbow, Kwok squatted down at the pig's rear end and dug his heels into the ground. He formed a point with the fingers of his right hand. Then he took a deep breath and pushed them into the pig. Slowly, his hand went in, twisting a bit, and then his forearm. The pig's inside gripped him like a wet, warm sleeve. He probed gingerly along the folds and edges until he touched the soft firmness of a piglet. Grasping it gently, he pulled out. Like a mashed white ball, the tiny animal lay silent in his palm, stained with blood and glistening with mucous.

Kwok quickly wiped his hand on his pants, then cupped the piglet carefully and rubbed it vigorously with the rag Lee Bing held out to him. The newborn wasn't as big or as well formed as others Kwok had seen.

Suddenly the piglet convulsed and started wheezing soft desperate breaths. The old man chortled like a child. Kwok looked for a dry spot to put the creature down. "Get some clean boards," he ordered.

Then he reached into the heaving mother pig again, repeating the bloody search over and over, pulling out soft, still bundles that Lee Bing rubbed to life. Finally Kwok's fingers did one last cautious sweep inside and came out empty. He sank back on his haunches and stared at the seven piglets, now pushing and tripping over one another as they struggled to hold onto their mother's slippery round teats for milk. He got to his feet, cleaning his hands again.

Lee Bing sounded shaky. "Wah, I was so scared," he started. "Thank you, Kwok. Thank—"

Kwok stopped him. "You should have fed her more when she got heavy. Feed her some warm slop tonight. Keep them dry and warm and clean. And get someone to help you clip their teeth."

"Yes, yes, I know about the teeth." Lee Bing nodded eagerly. "They showed me how to do all that, but not what you just did. Wah, who would believe this? Reach inside the pig with one hand to help the little things get born."

As Kwok headed home, his eyes narrowed against the unexpected glare of the afternoon. Good thing his feet could take him home on their own over the familiar trail. The birthing had exhausted him. Now he wondered if it had been worthwhile. At least half the piglets would die, if not all of them. The pig pen wasn't dry enough to keep away disease and trouble.

Kwok glanced down at himself. His hands and arm were smeared with blood and mucous. The greasy spots from the pig slop had darkened into permanent stains on his clothes. Mud clung to his knees. He shrugged. At least he knew how to handle the pigs. He had been quick and competent. Not even Ba could criticize his work, he knew that.

When Kwok strode into the family barn, their pigs rushed at him noisily, poking long snouts through the fence like anxious prisoners.

"All right, sorry I'm late!" he shouted. He grabbed the pails and went outside to pump water. Back inside, he filled the water trough. He threw some into the pigs' faces and laughed as they snorted impatiently. Ba had unloaded the slop tubs from the truck. Kwok mixed in generous amounts of dry feed, stirring it deftly with a shovel. Then he dragged the pail into the pen and filled the feeding trough.

"Enjoy this, porkers!" he cried. "If only you knew what hell it took to bring this home to you."

The four pigs swarmed around and shoved their faces into the mash of food, smacking and snorting as if it were their last meal. While they were occupied, Kwok cleaned the pen quickly with a shovel and pitchfork, pitching clods of manure into the wheelbarrow and swabbing straw around to mop up the dark streaks. Then he brought in more water and threw it across the rough-hewn plank floor. The manure and dirty straw he trundled outside to the growing pile of compost.

Now the spinach needed weeding. It had been a week since he had checked. He grabbed a basket and hoe and headed out. The light was beginning to fade, and seagulls swooped high above, cawing forlornly. The long rows of sprouting leaves twitched in the wind, bright green against the dark soil. The spinach was maturing quickly, thanks to the recent rainfall. The first crop would be ready in about three weeks. Kwok reminded himself to sow another crop in the unplanted rows.

He knelt and saw dark prickly stalks of weed-grass pushing through the soil. He grabbed them at the base and tugged gently. Long wispy roots slid out. He groaned. This was going to take a long time . . .

When he next looked up he saw Ying, his older sister, walking towards him. Her rubber boots and baggy overalls, patched and reinforced at the knees and the seat, were splotched with mud. She was a thin girl, as tall as Kwok, with large eyes and a pale, drawn face.

"Ma says get inside and start studying," she said, poking at the dirt under her fingernails.

Kwok went on working. He wanted to finish the row.

Ying squatted down beside him. "You've been out here a long time. It's almost dark."

Kwok shrugged. He had lost track of time. For the past two hours he hadn't once thought of Lee Bing and his pigs, Head Cook at his soccer game, or Ba and his tubs of slop. When he straightened up he had to arch his torso backwards to unlock the stiffness gripping him.

Kwok strode towards the house, and Ying followed. She untied the bandanna around her head and shook her hair loose into the wind. "The neighbours are coming here after dinner," she said. "To talk about the dykes."

Kwok groaned. How could he study if the old codgers were going to sit around and mouth off all night?

His sister's face crinkled. "You stink! What's that awful smell?"

Kwok walked on awhile before speaking. "We were pouring pig slop into the tubs behind the Chung King when Ba let go. I got drenched in it."

Ying clucked sympathetically. "Accident?"

"Better be."

She hesitated before asking her next question. "Do you have some spare time tonight? I'm having a bit of trouble with my chemistry homework."

An impatient sigh escaped from Kwok before he could help it. "A lot?"

Ying shook her head. "Never mind," she said quickly, pushing past him. "I'll manage on my own."

History was the least favourite of Kwok's courses. He skimmed through the textbook. Sir John A., Upper Canada, Lower Canada, Canada East, Canada West, the Durham Report—they were all a jostle of names and dates. Kwok wanted to understand it. After all, Canada was his home. But the pieces would not register in his mind the way chemistry equations and mathematical formulas could be memorized and applied. Now he sat at the table writing out a chronology, starting in 1763 and listing dates, events and results.

The Wong house had four rooms. In the middle was the biggest, with a wood-burning stove, tin-foil sink and a sawhorse table right in the centre. Around it, the family ate, studied, sewed, sorted seeds and worked through hundreds of other tasks. On either side of the main room were two bedrooms, one shared by Ba and Ma, the other by Kwok and Ying. Behind the stove was a small room used for bathing and washing. The outhouse was a short walk away.

Forty years ago, Grandpa and his four partners had built the house with heavy planks salvaged from the nearby mill. The shack failed to keep the cold out, so the following summer they had plastered the interior to seal it. The five men had slept on sawhorse beds pushed against the walls in a semi-circle around the stove. When Grandpa died, Ba bought out the partners, and then he and Ma put up walls to divide the house into the smaller rooms.

Now Ma brought over chopsticks and plates and began to set the table for dinner. She had washed and put on a clean dress and apron. Kwok started to close his book, but she stopped him.

"Read on," she said loudly in Chinese. "Not eating yet."

But Kwok shut the textbook firmly. He felt too hungry, too restless to work anymore.

Ma poked him sharply. "I said, go on studying." She looked small and frail, but determination flashed like knives in her eyes whenever she argued. In the wedding portrait that hung over the sink by the clock, she posed demurely. Eyes of a phoenix, brows of a swan, that's how Ma said men would describe her best features. In her younger days, her face was shaped like a heart, with dimpled cheeks tapering to a dainty chin. She had been one of the prettiest servant girls in Chinatown.

"You don't look at your books, for sure you'll fail," Ma warned. She had dampened her hair and rolled the short strands into circles, pinning them so that they would dry with a curl.

If only he had a table and lamp in his room, Kwok thought, then he could shut her out and get some work done. He snapped back. "I know how to study. Don't tell me what to do!"

"Your father's washing up. As soon as he comes out, we'll eat." Ma was used to Kwok's outbursts. She dropped a porcelain soup spoon onto each plate with a clang. "Go on, look at your books."

Kwok opened his book, but his mind was threading through schedules. Two weeks until the history exam, then the chemistry test came a week after that. That meant finishing the problem sets by the end of the week. Then there was half a textbook to review for biology. Good thing there wasn't any major new studying for math or English. He had to do well to make sure the soccer scholarship was his.

He was dreading school the next day. For sure Phil Scott would tell everyone how Ba had shouted and pushed and demanded payment over the almost accident. There would be a lot of laughing over that. It wouldn't be the first time that Kwok was the butt of ridicule.

"What sound does a Chinese duck make?"

"Kwok-kwok-kwok!"

His eyes passed dully over the room. Clotheslines strung along the walls held drying overalls and shirts. Ma tried to wash on clear days so that she could hang the wash outside, but there had been too much rain lately. To one side was his mother's old foot-treadle sewing machine; it doubled as a table when folded up. Underneath the sink, the rough wooden shelves were stacked with enamel wash basins, pots, tin cans and dishes. Ma never invited her old friends from Chinatown to visit, and Kwok knew why. Farm smells could prick strong and sharp in the heat of summer, but the smell of poverty stayed all year round. Ma hadn't wanted to move out here, but Ba had been determined to work the land his father had left him.

Ba strode in from the washing room, wiping his face vigorously on a towel. His long arms and legs stuck out from a shirt and pyjama pants that had shrunk from relentless washings. Tonight he was also wearing the woolly sweater Ma had knit for him. It still held a new shine. Obviously he didn't intend to go back out to work tonight. He sat down at the table while Ma hurried to stoke the fire, calling for Ying.

Noisily Kwok piled his books and papers up and took them away. He bumped into his sister at the bedroom door. When he came back to the main room, the stove crackled with the sound of frying vegetables. Ying walked gingerly to the table, carrying a steaming pan by its rim. Warily, Kwok sat down across from his father. Ba kneaded the back of his neck with his knuckles.

"Lee Bing's pig, how is it?" he asked.

Kwok watched him for a second before replying. "All right. Seven lived, two died."

Ba responded slowly. "You pull them out?"

Kwok grunted and Ba nodded. "Lee Bing was lucky to have you help him," he said. Then he shook his head. "Think he can raise them?"

"I told him to make the place clean."

Ma came to the table with a steaming platter of greens.

Ba's head lifted. "Wah, such good dishes!"

Kwok sniffed like a puppy. Ma had steamed a thick salty-egg custard with ground pork and water chestnuts, simmered a herbal chicken soup, and fried green beans with beef and black beans. Usually they only had salt fish and boiled vegetables with the rice. Maybe Ma wanted to freshen the house with food fragrances for tonight's visitors.

Ying brought over individual bowls of rice and then, in unison, everyone picked up a spoon and dipped into the soup tureen.

"This soup is good for you," Ma proclaimed. "Drink it while it's hot. You, too, Ying."

Kwok slurped loudly and seized his chopsticks, shoving meat and rice into his mouth until his cheeks bulged like a squirrel's. Then Ma announced gaily, "Today, it's Ying's birthday."

Kwok glanced at Ying from behind his bowl. She wore a new dress that he had not seen before. Ying didn't think too highly of Ma's home sewing, but there were few other choices. New clothes and a nice meal were the only birthday traditions in the Wong household.

"You're not a little girl anymore," Ba said loudly. "You have to start behaving like a grown-up now."

Ying nodded, her eyes lowered.

"Sorry. I forgot," Kwok muttered to his sister. He felt like kicking himself.

She shrugged. "Don't worry. I'll forget yours, too."

"Thanks."

"Any time."

They had to be mindful about how much English they spoke. One of Ba's rules was that only Chinese could be spoken at home. Long ago, when the children had started English school, Ba muttered, "I don't worry that you won't know any English, but

I do worry that you won't know any Chinese."
When the family moved out of Chinatown to the
farm, the rule came along with them. "We don't
live in Chinatown anymore," Ba had said, "but
we're still Chinese who speak our language."

"Twenty means you're an adult," Ma said
brightly. "So today is special."

"I'll help you with your homework," Kwok
whispered to Ying.

Ying was two years older than Kwok, but she
was still in grade eleven. Ba took her out of school
every spring and fall to help with planting and har-
vesting, so she missed weeks of classes. But Ying
always insisted on returning to school, repeating
courses over and over, and it was by her own will
alone that she had clambered out of grade eight,
grade nine and then grade ten. She had suffered
being the oldest, the tallest and the loneliest girl in
all her classes. Kwok, on the other hand, stayed in
school straight through because Ma insisted that
her son graduate. Ba would have prefered both his
children working beside him, building up the family farm without having to hire help.

The Wongs proceeded through the rest of dinner
in their usual fashion, eating rapidly and speaking
sparingly. As the dishes emptied, Ma fired up the
stove and seared the rice crust sticking to the cooking pot. When it started smoking, she poured in
water, igniting a burst of steam. The singed rice
flavoured the water, which finished off the meal.

After the table was cleared and wiped clean,
Kwok brought his books back to the kitchen for

another attempt at history. Ying took hot water off the stove to wash the dishes while Ma hurried to fix her hair. Ba lit his pipe and puffed by the stove, waiting.

When the neighbours were heard stomping on the porch outside, Ba opened the door. Kwok closed his books, but Ma beckoned him over to her sewing corner. She had cleared space for him where the light was good. Then she went to welcome the visitors.

Lee Bing, Choy Ning and Soo Yin looked as if they had just walked off their fields. Mud was caked on their jackets and overalls, and their boots were stained and wet. They pulled off their caps and called out to Ma with the customary greeting, "Have you eaten?"

Kwok and Ying greeted them formally as elder uncles. Ba sat them down around the table, and Ma opened a package of salted crackers and laid out mugs of Chinese tea. Then she disappeared into her bedroom.

Choy Ning was usually smiling and friendly, but tonight he started off without any of the usual pleasantries. "That bastard Drysdale wants to raise the rent."

Everett Drysdale was a businessman who owned most of the farmland on the north shore of the river. Except for Ba, all the Chinese farmers leased their plots of land from him. Originally from a pioneer farming family, Drysdale had become one of the city's biggest property owners. In the current Depression, he was buying up land and houses at bargain prices. Too many people had lost their jobs and couldn't maintain their payments.

Kwok had opened his textbooks on his knees. He didn't want to hear the men bleating and complaining, but there was nowhere else to go. He kept his head down and pretended to study.

Soo Yin fidgeted with his overall bib. "Don't know where he thinks we'll find the money. There's no gold in the mud here."

Ba asked, "Can you talk him down?"

"That bastard?" Choy Ning slammed his fist on the table. "Richest man in town, what he does he care?"

"You're lucky you own your land," Lee Bing remarked to Ba.

"Weh, I'm in debt, too. I owe that broken-leg Taro Head," Ba said drily. "I just told him that I'd miss this month's payment."

"He let you?"

"What's he going to do?" Ba asked. "Run out here and rip out my asparagus?"

Choy Ning sipped at the hot tea and shook his head. "Ah-Hoi, you're crazy. Borrowing money to buy land and seeds to start a crop of asparagus. Times are bad now. All around the world, not just here."

Ba leaned back, tipping his chair onto its back legs. "Prices are bad on everything. Everyone grows the same things all the way up the river to Hope. Carrots, lettuce, spinach, potatoes. The only way to get good money from the wholesaler is to grow something he can't get somewhere else."

"You think we don't know that? But asparagus takes three years!"

"Besides, you've got children to help you. You're the lucky one."

"The stupid boy has to study and write exams," Ba exclaimed. "Useless!"

Kwok refused to look up. Ba criticized Canadian schooling and the younger generation every time he had an audience.

"Not so," protested Lee Bing. "The only way to move ahead is to get an education."

Soo Yin chimed in, "You remember the proverb, 'In books and scrolls, there's jade and gold.'"

"That's in China," Ba said flatly. "Here you can have twenty university degrees and still they won't give you a job."

"There's no justice here, that's the problem," Lee Bing asserted. "You work all your life — forty, fifty, sixty years, and you have nothing to show for it."

"But what can you do?" Choy Ning was in a philosophical mood tonight. "The weather's bad, is that our fault? There's war in China, is that our fault? The whites hate us, is that our fault?"

"Who said life was easy?" Ba asked.

But Choy Ning wasn't finished. "The river is rising, is that our fault? Now it looks like the dykes won't hold. I've no cash. No one will lend me a cent. I don't have any money for repairs."

Ba and the farmers along this stretch of the river always pooled their resources to fix the dykes. It was cheaper to do all the work at once instead of piece by piece.

Lee Bing sounded hesitant. "Maybe the river will drop. Maybe we can wait until next year."

But Ba shook his head. "If it floods, we lose everything. I say we fix the dykes."

"Ah-Hoi, with what?" Soo Yin spoke plaintively. "With what do we fix them? I'm like Ning, I can't even scrape up half a cent. Where will you get money, Ah-Hoi?"

Kwok's ears perked up at this vital question, but Ba only grunted. Kwok didn't think there was any money. They had borrowed from Taro Head to buy the asparagus field, they had borrowed from the bank to pay land taxes, and they owed the supply store for seed, feed and fertilizer.

Choy Ning spoke slowly and rubbed his hands as if he were cold. "Maybe it's time to head home."

Lee Bing seemed surprised. "Back to the village? To China?"

"What would you do there?" Ba asked.

Choy Ning shrugged. "Who knows? A bit of this. A bit of that."

"You'd be with your wife," Soo Yin pointed out.

"But what about your debts here?" Ba demanded.

"I should be with my family," Choy Ning said, and the other men nodded in agreement.

Ba sighed. "So we're defeated, eh?"

Soo Ying shrugged. "If it floods, I'll go work at my cousin's farm. He's in Surrey, far from this damned river."

Ma came over with a tea kettle that had been roosting on the stove and filled everyone's mug with hot tea. But the conversation had lost its energy. Shortly, Choy Ning and Soo Yin stood up to go because they had a long distance to travel. Soo Yin came over to Kwok and nudged his knee. "You're lucky, Kwok. I wish my son were here to inherit this land."

Kwok nodded politely, but his mind was seething. I don't want this land. No thanks.

THREE

THE whistle shrilled loud and clear for half-
time, and Kwok stopped running. He caught
his breath, then jogged slowly towards the sidelines,
bracing himself. He hadn't felt so worried about a
game in a long time.

Mack and Taylor ran up from behind. "We . . .
are . . . mess . . . ing . . . up, in . . . an . . . awful . . .
way," Taylor said, huffing between each word.

Kwok listened to their boots plodding in squishy
unison over the mud and gravel, wondering if he
should speak. Taylor was a fair player but reckoned
himself much better.

Kwok slowed and let the others go ahead. The
rain had stopped, so the forest of umbrellas around
the field had fallen. Clusters of loyal South Hill
School fans were huddled along the sidelines. They
clapped and cheered as the team came in, even
though the score was 1-0 for the other side. It
looked as if half the school had come out. Kwok
even saw Miss Wilson and Miss Stirling, the school
secretaries, laughing and waving in their chic round
hats, short skirts and shimmery white stockings.
They were the ones that the girls watched to see if
hemlines were going up or coming down. Kwok
remembered when Mrs. Crowe the librarian had
complained about the lipstick and facial cosmetics

42

the younger women were using. Mrs. Crowe dressed like Ma, in long shapeless dresses, and she never came to soccer games.

"We are messing up," Taylor said again as the team gathered. Under a sheen of sweat, his face had reddened from exertion to match the carrot colour of his hair.

Kwok looked away. Behind him, South Hill's stately brick building gazed over the playing field. The Red Ensign clung soddenly to the flagpole. On the other side of the field came loud chants of "Team! Team! Team!" and "Win! Win! Win!" Their opponent, Central High, always travelled with a jubilant cheering section.

Around him, the players argued loudly.

"Yeah, we need Phil now!"

"Where's the captain when we need him?"

"It's a rough slog out there, isn't it?" Major Gale wrung his hands like a nervous banker and smiled weakly. He was the school principal. His hat and coat and face were soaked with rain, while an umbrella hung unused in the crook of his arm. The team straggled into a loose circle around him. Everyone was streaked with mud and rain and per-spiration. Some reached for towels, but Kwok squatted and waited.

He felt sorry for Major Gale. The principal came to every game and supported the team tirelessly, but the boys gave him little respect. Kwok had watched Taylor and the others imitate Major Gale's British accent and the peculiar way he tugged at his mous-tache, as if it itched.

This was a must-win game. For the first time in its history, South Hill had qualified for the high school league play-offs. Kwok thought it would be useful to have a league title listed on his school record. It might prove valuable some day. But if they lost today, they would be eliminated from the series.

"They shouldn't have scored," Taylor whined. "We let them dance in like ballerinas."

"So where was our defence?"

"Major Gale said to play up, to cover for Phil."

The players rolled and flexed on the balls of their feet. Usually at this time, Coach Carrothers would discuss the game and set strategy for the second half. But his wife had died two days ago, so Major Gale stepped in to help. Unfortunately, he had never coached before, and there was no one else. South Hill was a small school far from the downtown, a hick place out in the sticks.

"No use crying over spilled milk, boys," said Major Gale. He looked around nervously. "Let's see what we can do."

The team glared at him as he cleared his throat loudly. "I think you are doing splendidly, boys, considering your coach and captain are both absent." He paused. "We need the ball. We cannot score if we do not run with the ball."

The whole team sagged at the grim realization that Major Gale couldn't help them. They needed Phil. This was the worst possible game for him to miss. But for Kwok, as long as Phil stayed away, so would the news about Ba's stupid antics around the truck accident. It had been almost a week.

"What's wrong with you and Mack?" Taylor jabbed an elbow into Kwok. "You guys up front aren't even near their goal!"

Kwok glared back, angry that Taylor hadn't mentioned Jones, the other forward. Jones was another buddy of Phil and Taylor's, another one of the gang that chummed around together in the lunchroom and hallways.

Major Gale broke in apologetically, "It'll take time for Mack to get used to—"

"Mack's doing all right!" Kwok blurted. Eyes flickered at him, surprised. Kwok never said much to the team, so how could he contradict the principal in public?

Taylor snickered. "Oho! The rock speaks, at last."

Kwok forced himself to keep talking. "Mack, when you get the ball, move. Run or pass. Don't let the marker get to you."

The major concurred eagerly. "That's right, stand still and you're a sitting target."

Kwok spoke quickly, glancing nervously around the circle of hardened faces. "You know what's happening? Ever since Central scored, they're not taking chances. They're not sending men up."

He paused to see if anyone would disagree. The fellows looked as if they were trying hard to think. "They're not a strong team. That's why they're hanging back and playing defensive."

The players sneaked glances at the major, but he was nodding encouragingly, his eyeglasses glinting up and down.

Kwok continued, "If we want to win, we have to break them up."

"We have to score," Taylor countered sullenly. "That's what I want to know. Are we going to score?"

Kwok stopped. Why not let Taylor take charge? he thought wearily. He wants to be the big shot. Why stick my neck out? If things go wrong, I'll get all the blame. What do I know? I'm not team captain. I just want to win. It's a waste to play all season and come all this way only to lose just because we're so disorganized.

Kwok pressed his lips together and stepped back, but Major Gale called out, "Kwok, what would you do if you were coach?"

"Open up our attack," Kwok replied instantly. "When we cross the centre line, take the ball out to one side and play it there. Whoever's free goes for the other side, and— "

"And we send the ball across, from one side to the other, right?" Jones broke in as if he could see the play.

"And their goalkeeper's not that fast."

"But they're marking you and Mack all the time."

"It doesn't have to be us three. Anyone can run the ball up," replied Kwok. "Everyone attacks, all right?"

"This won't do a rap of good!" Taylor stood outside the circle of players, arms crossed. "We'll be leaving our own goal wide open."

"They're not playing an offensive game," Kwok said in exasperation. "They're not taking any chances."

"They'll spot this miles away."

"You have a better idea?"

Jones stood up and started running lightly on the spot. "Sounds good to me," he said.

***

The whistle sounded and Kwok bolted to take the opening pass from Mack. He pivoted away from the opposition rushing at him and flicked the ball back to Jones. Then the whole team was moving into Central territory. Jones faked to lose his marker and kicked the ball hard, sending it down centre field.

Kwok saw the Central forwards bearing down, trying to cut off the pass. Taylor took the ball while Kwok swung out to the side, his marker shadowing him closely.

Jones came up behind Kwok and suddenly zig-zagged away. Kwok's shadow hesitated, leaving Kwok momentarily clear for a pass. Taylor saw the opening, saw that Kwok was clear, but instead he ran for the goal on his own. He faked his way by one defender, but was tackled by another who promptly sent the ball booming back towards the South Hill net.

Damn! Kwok raced back. He knew Taylor couldn't be trusted.

Now Jones had the ball, and two attackers were dodging him persistently. Kick it! Kwok screamed silently. The field's too wet for dribbling. Sure enough, a second later, Jones lost the ball, but Taylor recovered it and sent it flying high up over centre field.

Kwok raced over, his head twisted up, watching the ball. He trapped it and moved down. Jones was ahead so Kwok cleared it to him. The Central defence tightened in the midfield and Mack slipped towards the other sideline. Jones drove the ball farther up before sending it to Kwok. Instantly, defenders closed around him like a fist, but instead of going for the goal, he crossed the ball to Mack.

Mack knew exactly what to do. He slid through the hole and sent it into the high corner of the net. Shazam!

Kwok leapt up, arms held high. They were going to win this game!

***

Kwok dropped into the visitor's chair with a sigh of relief and stretched his legs out in front of the paper-strewn oak desk. He had tracked a large amount of mud through the hallway and into Major Gale's office, but he was too happy and too exhausted to care. After the game, even the principal had charged onto the field, arms upraised and waving like a madman, shouting, "We won! We won!"

And the rest of the school? This marked only the start of the play-offs, but when the final whistle blew, they streamed onto the field in one wave, chanting and cheering like a victorious army, "Tro-phee! Tro-phee!"

The final score stood at 2-1. Jones scored the winning goal, so the students heaved him onto their shoulders and bounced him around. Kwok was walking fast short circles to cool the fire burning his lungs when Major Gale pulled him off to his office.

Now Gale peeled off his soggy overcoat and galoshes. He sat down behind the desk, pulling his tie tight to his neck. Instantly he was transformed into the stiff and proper principal who patrolled the halls with hands locked behind his back, sharp eyes scrutinizing every face and every movement.

"You played a humdinger of a game, Kwok! That was very sound advice you issued at half-time."

Kwok shrugged away the compliment and passed an arm over his forehead to stop the sweat from trickling into his eyes.

"You should speak up more often," Major Gale exclaimed. "You see things in the game that the others don't. Why do you stay so quiet?"

Kwok shook his head. He was in no mood to begin to address this question.

"Kwok, South Hill has never fielded a winning team like this!" exulted Gale. Kwok had rarely seen him smile so much. "This school will finally receive some serious recognition in the city."

"Could you call me Clark, sir?" Kwok looked earnestly across the desk.

Major Gale arched an eyebrow. "What's this? A new name?"

"It's like this, sir." Words raced out of Kwok's mouth. "I'm a Canadian. I was born here. I speak English. I'm really not Chinese. So I should have a Canadian name."

The principal shook his head and leaned back. "You're Chinese as soon as someone sees you. When did you decide this?"

"When I filled in the application form for the scholarship. I thought it might help."

"But they can tell from your last name that you're Chinese."

Kwok shrugged and kicked at his own foot. "Well, I thought with an English first name, they might think I was more Canadian than Chinese. You know how badly I need this scholarship."

Major Gale coughed and cleared his throat. His knuckles rubbed circles into his moustache. When he looked up, Kwok's ears began to ring. Bad news was coming.

"Speaking of scholarships," Gale said crisply. "That's really what I wanted to talk to you about. Your application came back today. It was . . . rejected."

The news slid like ice blocks down Kwok's back. "But you were sure—"

"Yes, I was, but I was wrong." Gale tugged at his lower lip, annoyed. "You're not getting a university scholarship."

Kwok stared at the mud streaked like black veins on his leg. Same as the mud from the farm. Black as tar. That was going to be his whole life. Him and Ba and the pigs. His stomach lurched.

"Did they say why?" Kwok looked up painfully. "Was it my marks? You said they were very strong. You said they needed good soccer players and that the combination of the two meant— "

"The letter didn't indicate why."

Tell the truth, Kwok thought angrily. But Gale's face stayed impassive. Kwok stood up, but the principal reached over and stopped him. "What are you going to do?"

"Play ball," replied Kwok, turning away. "Jones and I are on the Selects. They're taking us to practice now."

"No, I meant after graduation."

Kwok gripped the metal doorknob so tightly he thought it would crinkle. He couldn't turn around. Gale waited.

"What *can* I do?" Kwok swallowed and exhaled into the smoked glass facing him. His voice quavered. "It's simple, isn't it? No scholarship, no money, no university."

"You can't give up, Kwok . . . er . . . Clark."

Kwok kept his shoulders square.

"Can you get a job, save some money?" Major Gale asked helpfully.

"No, sir."

"Are you sure? Maybe I can help you."

Kwok turned on him furiously. "Men are sleeping on the streets, do you know that? There are no

51

jobs anywhere! Do you know anyone who would hire Chinese?"

"How about China?" Major Gale put on a soothing voice. "The newspaper says they're training pilots to fight Japan. China wants an air force. You could make a career there."

Kwok shook his head. "I don't speak Chinese."

"Why, of course you do."

"It's a village dialect," Kwok said, irritated.

Major Gale's forehead wrinkled. "But that's where your people are from."

"Not me!"

Kwok yanked the door and slammed it behind him. He plunged through the gloomy hallway towards the entrance. What was the point of all this? What was the point of studying so hard? Just so you could tend pigs and pull weeds for the rest of your life?

He could hear Ba chortling, "Didn't I tell you? Soc-cah? Fah! A waste of time."

What about Coach Carrothers? He would think Kwok had failed, too. It was the coach who had changed Kwok's life. Three years ago, he had noticed that the grade nine boys kicking the ball around at lunch were fast and a bit too eager. He had sauntered over and challenged them. "You fellows good enough to play league?"

Confident shouts had greeted him, and he'd grinned. Kwok had been sitting alone under a tree pretending to read. Carrothers had divided the boys into two teams and frowned. "We're short." He looked around and called out, "Mr. Wong! Get over here!"

That was the start. Of course Kwok had played before, but only during athletics class. Joining the soccer team marked the first time in his life that any connection with boys of his own age had formed. It had made him hopeful.

Kwok smashed a hand into the heavy outer door and thrust it open. He took a deep breath of fresh air. Forget the scholarship, he told himself. At least you can still play soccer.

He looked up and saw a big truck approaching, bouncing along the gravel road. The hubbub from the field grew louder as Jones and his friends surged over. The sign on the delivery truck proclaimed "Bastion Cigarettes" in bright yellow stripes and bold red letters. The company's trademark was a medieval turret, seen on cigarette packages and billboards everywhere. As corporate sponsor, the company assembled players from schools throughout the city to form a Select team that would challenge all-star high school teams from other cities. The Selects were Vancouver's best high school players. Their pictures would even appear in the newspaper. This afternoon the players were gathering for their first practice.

Kwok bounded down the stairs. The door behind him opened and Major Gale poked his head out. The crowd surrounding the truck opened up. Jones had just climbed aboard.

"Throw the pig off!" someone shouted. "Ain't no mud hole here!"

Locker room chortles rose. "True-life men live with mud!" shouted Jones.

Kwok made his way to the back of the truck and reached up to pull himself aboard. The faces above were all familiar, faces he had met from opposing teams.

Then someone grabbed his shoulder. "Where do you suppose you're going?"

The words came from a wiry freckled fellow with oily red hair. Tobacco fumes reeked from him.

"I'm on the Selects," Kwok said. He began to swing himself up, but the man stopped him again.

"Mr. Bastion never said a Chinaman was on the team. You can't get on!"

Instantly the crowd fell silent.

Kwok was speechless. The next second felt like an eternity before words came out. "But . . . you had our names two weeks ago. Nothing was said then!"

"I'm saying so now! You ain't getting on!" The driver slammed the gate and strode off.

Kwok stood stunned. Then he turned and ran. But not before catching a glimpse of Major Gale darting back into the school, the door shutting behind him.

FOUR

"**Y**OU'RE a coward, you know that?"

Kwok barrelled along, head down like a battering ram, wishing he could slam his ears shut as easily as he could close the thick doors of the school. His canvas bag, heavy with books, banged from one side of his back to the other.

Not much forest had been cleared this far from town, but North Arm Road led to the bridge, so a few automobiles and trucks rumbled by. The road was gravel and there were no sidewalks. Ying cradled a heavy armload of books, but that did not stop her from running after her brother.

"You should stand up for your rights." Ying's hair flew behind her in long thin wisps. Without losing a breath, she shouted at him, "You ran like a scared little titmouse! Why didn't you say something?"

Say what? Kwok's brain spun with frustration and anger. Say I'm the greatest soccer player in town? Say I'm a Canadian, too, and I have a right to get on the same truck with everyone else?

"Don't you have any pride?"

"Shut up."

"Don't you have any self-respect?"

"Shut up."

"What about those so-called friends of yours on the team? Did they do anything?"

Kwok spun and seized her upper arm. He bit down the urge to hit her. "Shut up," he hissed.

"You're hurting." Ying's face suddenly contorted with pain. Kwok shoved her aside and her books thudded to the ground. Her face hardened as she knelt to pick up her belongings. When Kwok saw the awkward homemade dress smear with grit, words of apology swirled inside him. He stooped to help but she snapped, "Get away."

Kwok paused, and she whispered fiercely, "Get away, I said."

He backed off, then ran, heading for home. I'm no coward, he told himself defiantly. What could anyone have said? No one could have changed that driver's mind.

Kwok reached the crest of the hill and bounded down. A breeze from the river swept up and cooled him slightly.

I should have told that deadbeat driver he was making a big mistake, Kwok said to himself, told him that Mr. Bastion had already seen me play and wanted me on the team. Freckle Face was just a driver, what would he know? I should have jumped aboard, just to see what the others would have done. Those fellows know me. They've played with me. Would they have looked away? Or stood up for me? He kicked a stone high and watched it tumble and roll ahead.

A familiar rattle sounded from behind. He turned and saw Ying bouncing inside Lee Bing's old truck. Their neighbour was returning home from the wholesaler. His sister kept her eyes fixed firmly ahead.

Kwok watched the wobbly tires twist and careen over the uneven road and plodded on miserably.

To his side, the woods stood peaceful and calm. Bright green was budding on the deciduous trees. On happier days, Kwok often left the road here and swung through the forest, enjoying the crackle of twigs underneath his feet and the sweet aroma of pine trees. He would imagine that the Wong farm, with its chimney puffing up smoke and its crops blooming in orderly rows, was one of the few beacons of civilization in this wilderness.

What a fool I've made of myself, he thought angrily. The university must have laughed good and hard at my application. They must have thought, who does this Chinaman think he is?

Kwok sucked in his breath, gripping his sides tightly. The afternoon's humiliations were like lumps of hot coal in his chest. Suddenly he turned and smashed his canvas bag against a tree. It was tied tightly and the books were held securely inside. The bag fell back heavily, and he seized it and smashed it at the tree again and again. Finally, he turned and headed home.

He jogged along the dirt road and veered around the thicket of tall trees into the clearing. He had always been grateful that the Wong house did not sit directly at the foot of the hill in full view of people gazing down from the avenues. If anyone from school ever saw the shack he lived in, he would die of embarrassment.

Kwok stopped. Fresh tire treads stood out in high relief in the mud. A gleaming black automobile stood in front of the house. Long and box-like, it had plush seats in the back, curtained glass windows on all sides, and three sets of headlamps.

Hope surged through Kwok and sent him running. Maybe the university had changed its mind and sent a telegram. Maybe Major Gale had rushed over with the good news. Maybe someone had reported Freckle Face to Mr. Bastion, and he had sped over with apologies to take him to join the team.

He charged into the darkened farmhouse and landed in a cloud of sticky sweet hair oil. The visitor's back was long and broad, draped in a heavy coat. The head came around and Kwok saw a prominent nose and dark furry eyebrows.

"Mr. Drysdale?" Kwok looked around the room like a trapped animal. Ba leaned stiffly by the window, one arm propped against the wall, the other sunk into his overall pocket. Ma stood at the sink, shifting from foot to foot, hands held behind her as if she were hiding something. The conversation seemed to have ground to a halt.

Instantly, Kwok was on guard. "Good afternoon. What . . . how do you do?"

A crisp white collar framed Everett Drysdale's big red face. His enormous middle was flagged by a tie of rainbow colours.

He reached out and shook Kwok's hand vigorously. "Kwok-ken, young man, it's good to see you again."

Kwok glanced at Ba, who stared nonchalantly out the grimy pane of glass. Kwok wished his father would move back into the room so that Drysdale wouldn't keep glancing towards the dust and mud smeared on the window.

"Ba, what's the matter?" he asked. His mouth felt dry and panic suddenly knotted his stomach. Had there been an accident? Had land taxes been raised?

Ba shrugged without turning. "Tell him to leave," he said tersely in Chinese.

Kwok turned to his mother and asked in Chinese, "Ma, what's happening here?"

She bit her lips and shook her head.

Everett Drysdale's voice filled the room. "I came here to do business with your father." He smiled, and his big white teeth glinted in the low afternoon light. "I want to buy this farm."

Kwok's heart began pounding.

"I am willing to pay very handsomely," Drysdale continued. "A thousand dollars."

Kwok sucked in a breath. Dizzy images lurched through his head. A house with a red roof. Flower bushes blooming beside a sparkling white front door. A living room with a fireplace. A plush sofa and velvet cushions scattered all around. Electric lights. Ma wearing dainty shoes with her hair smartly cut and marcelled like downtown ladies.

A thousand dollars could buy a new automobile or a small house. It was a great deal of money.

Finally, a normal life was within reach. But the expressions on his parents' faces were more appropriate for a funeral.

Ba shook his head slowly. His arms crossed like heavy armour over his chest. "Tell him to leave. I have work to do."

He stalked by Drysdale and thumped onto the porch. Ma looked at Kwok frantically. Her hair had been flattened by her bandanna and she wore a pair of Ba's old overalls. She flashed a shy smile at Drysdale and a beseeching look at Kwok and fled.

From his vest pocket, Drysdale pulled out a sleek silver case and shook out a cigarette. He lit it slowly, watching the match flame burn down to his fingertips before snuffing it. Kwok watched, frozen in his place. Behind him, a single loud plunk sounded as a drop of water slipped through the roof leak and hit the tin pail beneath.

"Your father is a good man," Drysdale proclaimed, exhaling a cloud of smoke. "But he can be extremely stubborn. And stubbornness is a fatal flaw that transforms good men into fools."

Ba's no fool, Kwok's mind retorted. Just because you've got money and land—

"I did not start out in this life as a wealthy man," Drysdale continued. "My success did not come easily. Everything, my young friend, depends on timing. You must know when to buy and when to sell. And your father should sell now."

Kwok averted his eyes and watched the flies crawling on the table. Ma had left a bowl of rice under a mesh cover. "Why do you want our farm?" he asked. "You already own everything else on this side of the river."

"Farming is finished here," Drysdale announced with quiet finality. "You farmers are barely earning enough to meet costs. You borrow to buy seeds, borrow to buy fertilizer, borrow to pay the rent, borrow to pay the taxes. You are all eyebrow deep in debt. And you haven't repaired the dykes in three years."

Kwok swallowed hard. Drysdale circled the tiny room and set his foot up on the water barrel. "Prices are dropping. What are you getting for potatoes? Twenty dollars a ton? Two years ago, you got thirty, thirty-five a ton. What will happen next year? What if it floods? What about carrots, onions, beans? Prices are dropping on everything. People pay pennies for their food now."

"Not on asparagus," Kwok retorted. "And people have to eat."

"Ah, but you don't grow enough asparagus to make it worth your while." Drysdale smiled slyly. "Not yet, anyways. You have another year to wait. What happens this autumn if prices drop? Asparagus rates went up last year only because of the rust infestation."

"Prices will get better," Kwok insisted bravely, amazed that a high-stakes entrepreneur like Drysdale knew so much about farming.

Drysdale shook his head. "You're no fool, Kwok-ken," he said gently. "You're a good farmer, but you know better. You have eyes, you have ears. You see men walking the streets, looking for work, you hear people calling for a general strike. This Depression is deep and serious. And there's going to be war in China. Everyone in Chinatown will be sending money home. They won't be spending or eating fancy meals."

Kwok took a deep breath and asked again, "So why do you want our farm?"

Drysdale inhaled from his cigarette deep and long before answering. "I am building a golf course," he announced. "This farm sits right in the middle of my site."

Kwok shook his head, bewildered. Shiny steel golf clubs didn't fit with muddy farmlands and pigs. Then he recalled seeing Drysdale's picture in the newspaper holding a gleaming trophy at a movie-star tournament.

"I plan to create the finest greens on this planet right here." Drysdale strutted from one end of the room to the other. "A designer from Scotland saw the site and said it was perfect. Already he's working on plans and drawings. I will build a grand clubhouse here, with swimming pool, tennis courts, even riding stables. It will be more spectacular than any site in the world. People will come here from New York, London, San Francisco. The river flowing by, birds rising from the marshes, the new airport so close. I will bring in tax dollars our city council has never seen before!"

Kwok was drowning in Drysdale's words. The delta lands were perfect for golf. They curled long and narrow along the river; they were flat and fertile. Grass would grow thick and swift here. "But you just said the Depression was deep and serious."

Drysdale smiled. "The people who play golf aren't walking the street. Rich people stay rich, no matter what."

Kwok swallowed hard. "So you'll make millions. Why don't you give us more money?"

Drysdale lazily blew out smoke rings. "I started at six hundred and I went up to a thousand," he said ruefully. "I thought I could help your father out. I know he had to borrow to buy half of Seto's old plot last year."

Kwok winced.

"He says he won't sell." Drysdale shrugged and flicked ashes to the floor. "For now, anyways."

"Did he say why?"

"No." Drysdale winked at the eagerness in Kwok's voice. "Does your father ever give reasons for what he does? What do you think?"

"He . . . he likes to farm, I suppose."

Drysdale brayed with laughter. "A man likes to work eighteen hours a day? A man likes to work seven or eight days a week? A man likes to live in a hovel like this?"

Kwok reddened. "I don't know why," he muttered sullenly. "My father is old-fashioned."

"Perhaps you can change that." Drysdale came up close and his eyes bore like drills into Kwok. "Don't let him make a mistake. Think of your mother. She deserves more, doesn't she? You go to school, you read books, you know better. Will you talk to your father?"

He clapped Kwok's back in a friendly way and walked out of the house. Kwok heard his car start without any hand-cranking. He waited until Drysdale had driven well away before he dashed outside to look for Ba. He searched through the damp-smelling barn and the tool shed. He dashed into the stuffy greenhouse and peeked into the grunting pigsty.

"Kwok!" From afar, Ying was calling. They had gone to the new field. Kwok turned and raced over. Seven years ago, Old Seto had returned to China after forty years of farming. He had been a pioneer in the district, arriving with Grandpa even before the outlying municipalities had incorporated.

"When I die, I want to be with my close ones," he had told Kwok before leaving. He had wanted to bring his wife over, but the laws did not allow it. After he left, no one wanted the lease because it was mostly low-lying land reclaimed from the river. Overnight, weeds choked it and thickened like bramble. Then Ba purchased half the field from Drysdale last spring, stretched a thin fence to separate the properties, and cleared it for a crop of asparagus.

The Wongs were gathered at the edge of the field at the dyke. Old Seto's field jutted out into the river like a callous and was threatened by flood on three sides. When he was a child, Kwok used to run around the field, imagining that this land was his castle and the water formed a protective moat around him.

Ba was lying over the dyke. He had one arm stuck under the water. Kwok ran up to him. "Ba, why won't you sell?"

"Sell what?" Ying leaned forward on her hoe. She had pulled on overalls and her workboots.

"Didn't you hear? Drysdale wants to buy our farm."

"You're joking." She dropped her hoe and ran up to hear more.

"He wants to build a golf course here. With a knock-out clubhouse for the rich. Tennis courts, swimming pool, the best of everything."

"So when does it happen?" Ying asked eagerly. "How soon?"

There was a pause. Kwok tilted his head at Ba. "He said no."

Ying's face crumpled in disappointment and Ma looked away silently. Kwok tried to stop the despair from growing. "What's the matter here?"

"The river's high," his sister replied dully. "Old Seto's dykes are shaky. They were weak when he left and they've gotten softer. Someone should have fixed them last time we were doing repairs."

Ba poked into the dyke with a long wooden pole. Normally the river flowed well below the dyke, so the grass and weeds knitting the dirt mounds into lumpy solid walls were sufficient to hold the river back.

"Ba, leave it," Kwok pleaded. "You can sell this place. You won't have to worry about the dyke."

Ma called out nervously, "Ah-Hoi, be careful." She had a morbid fear of the river, not because it could sweep over and ruin the fields, but because of the ghosts of the drowned that might lurk beneath the surface.

Kwok turned to his sister. "What do you think?" he asked.

"Have to shore them up."

"No, silly. The golf course. Selling the farm."

"It's not up to me, is it?"

"Think of Ma."

Ba pushed himself up and flung mud from his forearms. "Not strong enough," he asserted. "We need to shore it up. Get planks, pound them deep, keep the river from hitting the dyke."

"Planks?" Kwok was momentarily numbed with disbelief. "Get them from where, Ba? We don't have any money."

"I'll get planks and we'll press them in deep, deep into the river bottom." Ba's eyes gleamed with determination as he looked out over the river.

Kwok cut in front of him. "Ba, listen. Sell the farm to Drysdale. We don't need to do all this work. Besides, you can't just shore up our half. What about Drysdale's side of Seto's land? If it floods, the river will shoot straight in from the other side."

Ba ignored him. Ma and Ying stood silent.

Kwok grabbed his father's arm. "Ba, Drysdale is offering a thousand dollars. You're rich. You can buy anything you want."

Ba looked Kwok squarely in the face and paused. "My father started farming here forty years ago. All he left me was this piece of land. Nothing else."

Kwok looked down and backed off.

Ba said, "I say no sale and that's that." He started picking up his tools.

"Ba, I didn't get the scholarship." Kwok threw out his news desperately. "The principal, he told me today."

His father stopped, and his face seemed to darken. "What did you expect? Whites to give university money to Chinese? Fah!"

And then he was striding away.

FIVE

K WOK banged the Model T's horn impatiently and sent out a piercing blast. Ying hopped out onto the porch, one arm stuck into the sweater dangling by her side, the other cradling a pile of books. The door thumped behind her as she thrust her foot into her shoe.

She was barely aboard when Kwok shot the truck out of the clearing. In a panic, the pigeons pecking for stray seeds fluttered away. The morning sky loomed low, grey and heavy, but Kwok could tell change was approaching with the salty breeze from the ocean. After school Ba wanted them to fetch the pig slop and have the truck repaired in Chinatown. He had nothing to deliver to the wholesalers today.

Tree branches scraped and tugged at them as the truck twisted through the narrow pathway to the road. Then they were climbing the long hill while the engine throbbed and complained. Ying cheerfully combed her hair and tied it with a ribbon.

"How's the studying?" she asked. "Have you figured out what the important people were doing a hundred years ago?"

She had seen Kwok's history books strewn across the table the night before. No one had spoken much after the stormy gathering atop the dykes.

Chores were done, dinner was swiftly eaten, and then Ba clumped back out to the greenhouse. Later, when everyone was in bed, Kwok heard Ma speaking to Ba in low, earnest tones. Kwok strained to hear, but every sentence was cut off by sharp words from Ba.

"I'm sorry you didn't get that soccer scholarship," Ying said brightly. "You'll still graduate on the honour roll, won't you?"

Kwok leaned forward to check the traffic. "Who cares? What's the use?"

Ying turned away and folded her arms across her chest. "You know who cares," she said bluntly. "You want to break Ma's heart?"

Kwok shifted gears and grunted as the road rushed at him. "I'll see."

"So when's the next game? And who do we go against?" Ying's sudden interest in the South Hill sports scene was entirely unconvincing. She volunteered in the library at lunch time and studied there after classes as late as she could before hurrying home to do her chores. Kwok reckoned she was finally feeling sorry for him after yesterday's humiliations.

"Friday," he replied.

Ying reached over and patted Kwok's shoulder reassuringly. "Well, don't worry. As long as a Wong is on the field, we'll win."

Don't bet on that, Kwok thought grimly. Give me a good reason to stay on the team. No university wants me to play for them. Bastion Cigarettes doesn't want me on their Select team. Why should I get wet and cold? Why risk breaking a leg? Why run onto a mucky field where everyone can boo and hiss at you like you're a criminal? Maybe Ba had been right all along. Maybe soccer was a waste of time.

Nearing the school, the Model T poked through straggling threads of students. The slowest ones trudged along as if half asleep. Boys tossed a ball back and forth, shouting and running onto the road. Two girls whispered to each other over their books and bagged lunches. Mack and Eleanor sailed by dreamily, swaying from side to side, their arms around each other's shoulders like thick scarves.

"When did they start going together?" asked Ying.

Kwok shrugged. He didn't pay attention to the pairings and chasings of his classmates.

The truck pulled alongside the school building where a handful of automobiles were neatly parked. With a loud spray of gravel, a sportster swung in behind, jerking to a sudden stop and honking loudly. Phil Scott jumped out and hurried towards them. Every golden hair on his head was neatly tucked into place. It must have been tennis day for him, because he was dressed from head to toe in white: long white pants with razor-sharp creases, white running shoes with white laces, and a white knit sweater over a starched white shirt.

Taylor got out and leaned on the other side of the car. Yawning broadly, he watched Phil reach out and shake Kwok's hand. "Hey, I hear you did great things for the team. Congratulations."

Kwok's mouth slipped open, but not a word came out.

"I had to go over to the Island for tests and interviews at the military college, but I didn't expect Carrothers to duck out on the game," Phil said. "Then I had to visit relatives for a couple of days. Good thing you were around to set things up. Thanks, champ."

He grinned and then ran back to Taylor. Ying and Kwok watched them disappear into the school building, their heads close together. Finally she nudged him. "Well, weren't those nice words from Mr. Wonderful himself?"

Kwok shook his head disbelievingly. Other than Major Gale, no one in the school had spoken a single word about the game to him. Until now. The sun suddenly broke through the clouds, casting the school in a furry yellow haze.

***

In Chinatown after school, Kwok and Ying parked the Model T in the alley behind the Chung King and hurried around to the front. They had stopped at the garage, but the shop was closed. Now, as they passed the greengrocer, Kwok paused and peered at the prices over the wrinkled vegetables. He shook his head. He couldn't imagine people buying such dry, shrivelled greens. If the farmers sold directly to the stores, the vegetables would be fresher, but it was easier to sell a truckload at once to the wholesaler, who in turn sold the stores what they needed. The farmers didn't have time to go from store to store, selling one or two crates here and there.

At the Chung King, Ying and Kwok shoved open the door and strode into the restaurant. They stopped abruptly. Head Cook stood at one of the round tables in the middle of the room. He was wearing a suit and surrounded by his waiters. Four Eyes sauntered around impatiently, as did Fat Boy and Joe, looking ill-tempered and angry. Choy, who always seemed to have a finger up his nose, clearing and cleaning his itchy nostrils, leaned idly against the counter.

Kwok didn't recognize the men right away because they weren't wearing the usual restaurant smocks. Instead, everyone wore street clothes: jackets, sweaters, collarless shirts, baggy pants, black shoes. Cloth caps and felt hats were piled on the table. There were no customers in sight.

Ying looked around, surprised. "Having a meeting?"

"Shutting the place down," snarled Four Eyes. "You two, what do you want?"

The two teenagers looked at Head Cook in consternation. They caught a downcast look of shame on his face. He sighed and nodded reluctantly. "That's so. Not enough business. So I'm closing down. Fifteen years it's been."

Kwok didn't believe his ears. "But last week you had lots of customers," he said. "You were busy cooking in the kitchen. There were two drums of slop left over."

Head Cook sighed. "People eat and don't pay. They say, put it on my account. Fifteen cents a meal here, twenty cents a meal there. It all adds up. What can you do? They're not strangers."

Ying sounded worried. "So what will you do?"

Before the owner could answer, his waiters had pulled him away.

"We'll go now," said Ying, turning to leave.

"No, wait for me," Head Cook called out after them. "I'll be fast."

Kwok and Ying retreated into a corner. They used to call Head Cook Uncle Yook. Fifteen years ago, he grew corn down by the river, on a piece of land not far from the Wongs. He and Ba were old drinking buddies who headed to Chinatown every weekend to visit the game halls. But Uncle Yook always brought back treats for the children: won-ton soup in a big tin can, soft red sweets that turned your pee pink, or coconut candies as hard as rock. The Ba he dragged back was sometimes so drunk he was sick or dead to the world.

Then Uncle Yook stumbled across a business opportunity to buy into the restaurant, and he left the farm with a big happy smile. Kwok never figured out where he had learned to cook.

Kwok averted his gaze from the meeting; his eyes fell upon the cash register with its till open and empty, the wall calendar with last month's page still undetached, and the rack with dusty packages of cigarettes. The potted plants in the window looked wilted. He groaned softly, thinking how the cost of feeding the four pigs at home would soon escalate.

Fat Boy crossed his pudgy arms across his chest as a war of angry voices raged around him. "When are our wages coming?" he demanded.

The other waiters cursed loudly.

"Three weeks' pay you owe us."

"Three-fifty a week makes it ten dollars and fifty cents each."

"Told him to close earlier but he never listens."

"Dreamer. Rock-brain."

"Wasted our time."

Head Cook threw down his cigarette and motioned for quiet. He shot his fingers through his bristle of grey hair. "I have plans to get the money," he announced. "I pay my debts, you all know that."

"You haven't got a cent," cried Choy.

"He thinks we're fools."

Calmly, Head Cook let the clamour die. Then he said serenely, "I took every cent I had, I pawned my radio and I pawned my watch, and I bet it all on the Chinese Soccer Team in today's game."

The moment of silence was squashed by a loud explosion of fury as the men thumped and banged the table.

"Flushing money down the toilet would be easier."

"The team can't win. They're losing members every week."

In the shadows, Kwok and Ying wriggled uncomfortably.

Head Cook shook his head. "They won their last two games. Besides, it's better than nothing. After the game, come see me. Now get out of here."

"What if the Chinese team loses?" demanded Fat Boy.

"We won't lose," Head Cook said firmly. "We're headed for the Northwest Trophy."

"If you don't pay me," threatened Choy, "I'll break in here and cart off all your pots and tables and chairs and sell them for cash. I'm telling you straight, hear?"

"Oh, just get out, all of you," Head Cook said jovially. He didn't seem worried at all.

The men snatched at their hats and sprang to their feet, overturning and kicking the chairs aside like bad-tempered children.

Head Cook came to Kwok and Ying. "Your truck's out back?"

Kwok nodded.

"Then drive me to the park. The game's already started," he said excitedly. "Today, it's the last game of the season. We're up against the Canadian Canning Company. If we win, we play for the Northwest Trophy."

Kwok could hardly refuse. Over the years, Head Cook had donated tons of pig slop to the Wongs.

Head Cook pulled the tattered shades down over the windows and locked the front door. They padded through the dim, deserted kitchen, where a pungent smell lingered. All the dishes and pots had been washed and dried and stacked away.

"Why don't you sell this stuff?" Ying asked.

"You've got lots of dishes here. Maybe someone else wants to start a restaurant."

"If I sell now, I'll hardly get any money," Head Cook replied. "But if things improve I might get a better price. Or maybe I can reopen and start cooking again. Nobody makes sticky-rice chicken like I can."

Out in the alley, Head Cook hurled his body against the heavy door to shut it. He jumped aboard the truck, grinning like a schoolboy just released for summer holidays.

"Cambie Street Grounds?" asked Kwok. Head Cook nodded eagerly as the truck rolled onto the street. There was hardly any traffic, even though it was the middle of the afternoon. Everyone must be at the game already, Kwok thought.

"Your father, how is he?" Head Cook was squished tightly between the two teens.

Ying replied woodenly, "Fine. You're kind to ask."

"How's the new field of asparagus coming along?"

Kwok quickly answered, "Good, good. A lot of work. You know how it is."

Ying nudged the cook. "Will you farm again?"

He shook his head. "No, too old for that. I can't bend my back like before."

"Then how will you manage?"

Head Cook shrugged. "Don't worry, I'll get by." He saw Ying's troubled expression and smiled. "Oh, Ying, don't make such a long face. Now I can go fishing. How about that? Haven't gone fishing in years. And then I can come down and visit you. And Lee Bing's pigs."

They all chuckled.

Head Cook continued. "I hear he's going to build a barn for his new family."

"But he doesn't have a nickel," Kwok exclaimed.

"Taro Head will lend money to a two-year-old if he can charge enough interest," replied Head Cook. "Lee Bing will build it himself, he says."

Kwok sputtered in disbelief.

"It's true," Head Cook said. "He's going to buy the lumber and start soon. These days, he's calling the piglets his children."

The truck chugged up the Pender Street hill. To one side, in Victory Square, dozens of men sat idly or lay sleeping on the grass and stone benches surrounding the war memorial. Some were reading newspapers; others played chess and checkers. These days the jobless had made the park their home. It was close to the docks, the railway tracks and the hotels of Skid Row.

From there the playing fields were only a short distance away. On Cambie Street automobiles and trucks were parked everywhere, some on the sidewalk, some half on the road.

"Come watch for a while," Head Cook said.

Kwok and Ying hesitated. At home the farm chores waited like the ticking of a clock.

But Head Cook waggled his head and chuckled. "Farm work never ends," he told them. "You finish one thing, there's always something else waiting. If you find a free minute and don't use it, it's your loss."

They jumped out of the truck and hurried towards the field. Ying smoothed her skirt and pulled at the tangles in her hair. Head Cook ran ahead to see where the Chinese were gathered.

The field was empty, though the bleachers and sidelines bulged with noisy spectators. A crowd of Chinese teenagers was spread over several rows in one high corner. Some of the girls had their hair cut very short in the popular flapper look. Others tied back their long hair simply like Ying did. Kwok tried not to stare at them. All the Chinese teenagers laughed and called to each other loudly as if the park were their own living room. Ying drew close to her brother as they fought their way through the crowd.

Kwok scanned the grass thickly carpeting the pitch and the lines clearly laid with thick dustings of chalk. He and Ying slowed as they approached a large crowd of Chinese. Words and phrases in Toisan dialect buzzed by them. Curious eyes lingered on them, like the cigarette and cigar smoke that hung everywhere. Across the field, most of spectators were white.

When they finally found a spot to stand, Kwok stepped forward and looked down the field. On the sidelines the Chinese players hopped up and down on their toes and flung their fingers about to keep loose. He glanced at the teenage spectators behind him. They had food with them: orange slices and white steamed buns were being handed up and down the rows. Suddenly his stomach growled. Have to go soon, he thought. Work to do. The weeds. Thin the carrots, check the asparagus field. Second seeding of lettuce coming up—

"I thought Head Cook said the game had already started." Ying sounded suspicious.

"Kwok, there you are." Head Cook ran up and seized Kwok's arm. One of the soccer players from the Chinese Soccer Team was behind him. "This is T.C., the team captain."

T.C. was the smallest soccer player Kwok had ever seen, and he did not look anything like an athlete. His blue jersey hung loosely like a potato sack over his skinny legs. His hands looked raw and red, as if he had been washing vegetables all day. His face was dark and pock-marked by some scarring disease, but his eyes gleamed with game fever. He smiled briefly at Kwok, revealing a jag of crooked teeth.

"I saw you playing the other day," he said briskly, shaking hands. "Against Central."

"You came all the way out to South Hill?" Kwok was surprised that someone who looked so old-country spoke such fluent English.

T.C. nodded. "Head Cook here told me that you were a razzle-dazzle player, so we went to see for ourselves."

Head Cook grinned at Kwok.

"I liked what I saw," T.C. continued. "Listen, would you consider joining our team?"

Kwok was so surprised he did not move.

T.C. frowned. "We're losing people. Ching Lee

just got a job up at Ocean Falls, and Wesley Chan is heading for China. We're running low on good players."

Kwok shook his head vigorously. "No. I wish I could help you, but I can't. Sorry."

Then he was swiftly pushing his way out of the crowd.

SIX

KWOK swished his grimy hands in water and dug at the mud under his nails with a small brush and metal pick. Dumping the dirty water down the drain, he mixed more hot water from the kettle into the basin. He quickly ran soap and a wet facecloth over his body, then he heaved the basin to the floor. Wrapping a towel around his middle, he sat on the stool and lowered his feet into the water. Instantly heat raced from his toe-tips to his forehead, and the weariness in his muscles and his mind began to melt.

Not a bad day, he thought, lazily watching wisps of steam drift to the roof. He had received compliments from two different soccer team captains. Back at the farm, the carrots had been thinned, the pigs fed and the weeding of the spinach finished. At lunch he had finished his listing for the history exam.

Now, he thought grimly, if only the university people could have observed him like T.C. had. Then they would have offered him a scholarship for sure. And if that Bastion Cigarette driver had seen him on the field, Kwok would probably be running with the Selects now. He wondered if the Chinese Soccer Team had won today's match.

He leaned back and rubbed his feet absently, wondering what playing for Chinatown might be like. The Chinese crowds were certainly noisy — fans who stayed until the last minute, supporters who never gave up hope. If he was a soccer star, he'd be able to look the other Chinatown teenagers straight in the eye. No one would laugh at him for being a hick farm boy.

"So why don't you play for Chinatown?" Ying had demanded on the way home, "You'd help them win."

"No."

"Why not? You were ready to play for the Selects."

"That was different. I knew those fellows. I'd played against them before. I don't know any of these people from Chinatown."

"So what? Get to know them!"

"But they're so . . . Chinese."

"You think you're not?"

Kwok had to grope for an answer. "We didn't grow up there. We didn't go to Chinese school. We're not like those people."

"What people?"

"Chinatown people."

Ying had rolled her eyes and given up on him after that. For the rest of the day, he had worked alone.

Now Ba could be heard in the other room, dogged by another man's voice. It didn't sound like any of their farm neighbours. Kwok dried his feet and hurried to the clean clothes that Ma had left neatly piled by the hot water kettles. The voice didn't belong to Everett Drysdale. Maybe it was his lawyer or some go-between arriving with another offer to buy the farm.

But the conversation through the door buzzed along peacefully.

When Kwok stepped into the main room, the air was pungent with the aroma of hot chicken broth. Ma swiftly sliced vegetables and meats at the sink, while a whole chicken, plump and freshly poached, sat cooling on the side. Tiny gold studs in Ma's ears caught the light, and her good green dress peeked out from under the long apron.

Kwok frowned. His parents must have come in earlier to wash up and change their clothes.

Ba called him over. "This is my son, Kwok-ken," he said.

The visitor reached out and they shook hands.

"This is Lee Dickson," Ba continued. "Editor of the Chinese Arrow newspaper."

Kwok looked at the guest suspiciously. Stout in a middle-aged way, Dickson exuded a shy but prosperous air with his pudgy build and soft face. He wore thick eyeglasses, a well-fitted suit and a dark blue tie. His shoes had been polished to a blinding sheen.

"I came to interview your father," he said in thickly accented English. He offered a friendly smile. "About how this Depression is affecting farmers."

Kwok shrugged and carried his books into the bedroom. He hoped Ba wasn't going to deliver his we-don't-speak-English-in-this-household speech tonight.

Ying sat on one bed, tying her hair back. She was wearing her new dress again. Kwok dropped the books on the other bed and lowered his voice. "Why would anyone want to interview Ba? Who is that fellow, anyways?"

Ying shrugged. Her teeth were clenched around some bobby pins.

"Ba doesn't even read the Arrow, the old fool," Kwok grumbled. The only newspapers Ba scanned were those that had been discarded for being weeks behind the time.

"You don't have to badmouth Ba all the time," Ying snapped.

Kwok wasn't listening. "I'll bet Ba wants to borrow money from him. That's why we're having chicken tonight."

Ying looked annoyed. "What do you care?"

"We can't afford to eat like this," Kwok retorted. "The cost of feeding the pigs is going up."

"Ying!" Ma called. "Come set the table for supper."

"Ba just wants money to fix the dykes," Kwok muttered as Ying brushed past him. How he wished his father would sell to Drysdale. That would put an end to pigs and weeds and mud. And they would have a bathtub with hot running water and a toilet that would be warm in winter and free of flies in summer.

He peeked into the kitchen. Ma chopped the chicken with loud whacks of her cleaver. Ba and

Dickson chatted at the table as Ying set out chopsticks, spoons and plates. A bottle of Scotch, newly opened, stood between the two men. Ba had rolled up his sleeves as if the meal were going to require a major physical effort. Dickson had taken off his jacket, revealing shiny leather suspenders. Ba wore the springy elastic kind, only they were loose and torn.

"The police raided another game hall yesterday night," Dickson was telling Ba in Chinese. "Arrested thirty people."

"Serves them right," exclaimed Ba. "In those places, they lose the few pennies they have left."

"But some of the men weren't gambling," protested Dickson. "They just wanted somewhere warm to sit down."

"They should go to the soup kitchen," Ba said, tossing back a shot of Scotch.

Ma brought over a platter heaped with glistening pieces of chicken and gaily invited them to start eating. "To accompany the liquor," she said.

Dickson stood up. "Let's wait for everyone. Here, let me help out."

As Ma called for Kwok, Dickson went to the stove where Ying was ladling out the broth and carefully carried the brimming soup tureen to the table.

"No, no, no." Ma ran after him in a fluster. "You don't have to do that. You're our guest."

Kwok sat down and delivered the bad news. "Head Cook closed shop today. Not enough business to keep going, he said."

"I asked him if he wanted to farm, but he said no," Ying interjected. "He said he wanted to come down and fish instead."

Dickson's eyes lit up. "Do you folks fish? I've always wanted to go fishing."

Ma dropped vegetables into the hot wok and steam crashed out. When the sputtering subsided, Kwok said, "Head Cook bet every penny he had on today's game to raise money for the waiters' wages."

"Good thing the Chinese won, then," exclaimed Dickson.

"The Chinese won?" Kwok asked.

Dickson peered at him over his glasses. "You like soccer?"

Kwok swallowed uncomfortably. "I hear the team is running short of players."

Dickson nodded. "Two fellows just sailed for China last week. They're going to join the Chinese Air Force to fight the Japanese. You ever think of doing the same?"

Kwok shook his head. "It's not my war."

Dickson looked at him wonderingly, and Ma hurried to the table with a dish of hot vegetables. "He's graduating this year," she said to Dickson.

Ba harrumphed loudly. "Waste of time. You can't get ahead here no matter how much education you have."

Dickson looked over at Ba, who swallowed another gulp of Scotch. "Haven't seen you at the soccer field."

Ba stuffed a piece of chicken into his mouth and chewed quickly. "Farmers don't have time to stand around and watch grown men chase a ball back and forth all day."

Ying brought over bowls of rice, and then everyone was politely inviting everyone else to start eating.

"All Chinatown watched the game today," Dickson said between mouthfuls. "The heads of the clan clubs, the teachers from the language schools, the church minister and his wife, even my mother and all her friends."

He laughed and Ma asked, "Your mother, how is she? I haven't seen her in a long time."

"She's fine. She told me to ask well of you. You knew her from long before, didn't you?"

Ma glanced at Ba. "I was a maid servant for the Hing Lung family. Your mother used to visit our First Lady all the time, bringing sunflower seeds for snacks."

Dickson looked at her intently. "You were just a child then."

"I worked there from age five until I was sixteen," Ma recalled. "You had been sent back to China for most of that time, I think. Your mother used to worry so much about you. She was always shipping tins of biscuits and knitting woollen vests for you."

"Your father was a rich man," Ba interjected. "Of course he'd send you to China for an education."

"I wish I had gone to school in Canada." Dickson's eyes looked sad for a second. "Then I could speak English like Kwok and Ying."

"I'll do anything to put my boy through university," Ma declared. "Otherwise why work like a donkey on this farm?"

Kwok flushed red with embarrassment. Dickson glanced at him. "As long as he gets away from this city, he'll do fine. Things are much better elsewhere in Canada."

Ba slapped the table and threw down his chopsticks. "Fah, no one hires Chinese, no matter how well you speak English. They take one look and bang goes the door."

An awkward silence ensued and Dickson turned to Ying, who had sat quietly most of the evening. "How about you? How is school going?"

Ying looked up hesitantly and said in a small voice, "Fine." She pushed rice into her mouth and chewed it slowly. Suddenly everyone seemed to be watching her. Finally she swallowed and spoke to Dickson. "You've come to write something about farming?"

Dickson nodded. "Rents are up, prices are down," he said. "All the farmers are heading back to China. Your father's a long-timer."

"If you hadn't brought this bottle along," Ba said jokingly, "I wouldn't even talk to you."

"It's nothing at all," Dickson laughed. "We're among our own, eh?"

"Not so," said Ba. "You're a man of words, you've got a position."

"You've got a lot of land," Dickson pointed out.

"I've got a lot of debt," Ba corrected him.

"Do you want to sell, then?"

Ba drew back in exaggerated horror. "Sell? Then what? If I sell, I'll have nothing. Is that why I came to Canada? To have nothing? I could have had lots of nothing in China."

He'll never sell, Kwok thought wearily, not in a million years. He went to the stove to refill his bowl with hot rice. Let Ba ramble on. Kwok had heard it all before.

"In China, that's where land is important," Ba said firmly. "But I had none, not even half a mou. My father left home, my mother died. I was a boy so I went to live with relatives. The uncle worked me like a water buffalo and fed me like a dog. Rice porridge twice a day. He owned land, but I worked it for him. I had no land, so I was a nobody."

"Now you own this big farm," exclaimed Dickson. "Those with no name can become land barons here."

Ba swore in Chinese. "Chinatown thinks nothing of farmers. The big-shot businessmen make big profits buying buildings, make bigger profits trading goods. They call you stupid for working on a farm." He paused. "But I don't pay them any attention. I work hard, I have land I call my own, I sleep well at night."

Dickson said softly, "You can make a lot of money if you sell your land to Drysdale."

"Like I said, I want to sleep well at nights." Ba pushed Dickson's elbow to make his point. "Land is for growing food, not for playing golf and other silly games."

Ma and Ying cleared the table and served tea and sliced oranges for dessert. Ba talked on and on. Dickson pulled out pencil and paper and scribbled notes. Prices had dropped while land taxes stayed the same. If a farmer grew too much, the marketing boards forced him to dump it. Chinese greengrocers stopped selling on Sundays to keep the white competitors from complaining to the politicians and newspapers. Many of Ba's farming friends had given up. One fellow tied a rope around his neck, threw the coil over the roof beam on his back porch and stepped off the railing. It was a week before they found his body.

Finally Dickson stood up and rubbed his eyes. "It's time to go," he said, smiling gratefully at Ba. "The young people need to study."

He thanked Ma profusely for dinner, shook Ba's hand, and then he was gone. Kwok went to the bedroom and brought his books back to the table. He stuffed the remaining orange slices into his mouth while Ba poured himself a sliver of Scotch and toyed with his glass, spinning the amber liquid around like quicksilver. He looked thoughtful. Ying brought her books out to the table, too, and took the leftover plates to the sink.

Ma whispered to Ying, "Your big day is approaching." She grasped Ying's hand and pulled her close. "Do you like him?"

The oranges suddenly soured in Kwok's mouth. His slight liking of Dickson evaporated instantly.

Ying shook Ma off and came back to the table. Kwok spat out the peel he been sucking on. "Ying is supposed to marry him?" he asked, incredulous.

The room fell silent as the clock over the sink ticked on steadily. Ying glanced at him. "It takes you a while to tie into things, doesn't it?"

"But he's too old for her." Kwok looked from Ma to Ba and back again in a panic. Their faces remained expressionless. "She doesn't even know him."

"Of course she doesn't know him." Ma came quickly to the table. "After they're married, they'll have lots of time to talk."

Kwok stared at his sister, waiting for an outburst. Instead, she turned the pages of her textbook as if nothing had happened. She read, wrote some quick notes and continued to read. Ma fetched the broom and started sweeping the floor as Ba swallowed the last of his liquor.

Finally Ying looked up. "We need the money," she said.

Kwok shook his head, not wanting to believe his ears.

Ying's fist lay tightly clenched on the table. "Ba needs the bride money to repair the dykes."

"I'll fix the dykes!" Kwok threw his pencil down. "I'll figure something out that won't cost— "

"And we need money for your university tuition," Ying added.

"My what?"

Ma stuck the broom under the table and swept vigorously. "If you're going to university, that's how it has to be."

"Then I don't want to go!" Kwok burst out.

"Fine," Ba interjected. "You don't want to go, fine by me."

Ma turned on Ba. "Don't listen to him," she said fiercely. "Of course he's going." Then she hissed at Kwok through clenched lips. "How dare you talk so stupidly? I didn't raise a son to clean pig pens all his life."

Ying reached over and covered her brother's hand with hers. "It was going to happen sooner or later."

"But it doesn't have to be like this." Kwok threw his hands up. "Don't you want to finish high school? You've worked at it so hard."

"Yes, but —"

"Silly girl won't need a diploma," Ba interrupted. "Dickson's got all the education you'll ever need. He can read and write Chinese. He's got a good job."

"He goes to church, too," Ma added. "And he has a nice house."

Ying forced a smile onto her face. "So what more could I want?"

"How can you marry someone you don't love?" Kwok persisted.

Anger suddenly flared in Ying. "You want me to fall in love? Who with? We live on a farm, we don't meet people, we don't know people. What should I do, run an advertisement in the daily news?"

"Don't get mad at me," Kwok said.

She grabbed the toilet paper by the door and ran outside. They heard her footsteps heading for the outhouse. Ba stood up and padded towards his bedroom.

"You're full of trouble." Ma poked Kwok's head with a finger. "This is none of your business. Who asked you to say anything?"

"It's not right."

"That's how it is," Ma declared. "Sooner or later, daughters have to leave home."

"Why can't she finish school first?"

"We need the money."

"She doesn't even know this man!"

Ma shook her head. "Back home, a girl doesn't see her husband's face until her wedding day."

"That's in China," Kwok said, exasperated. "This is Canada."

"Being a parent is like this." Ma spoke as if she were talking to herself. "What do children know about marriage?"

"But she doesn't know him," argued Kwok.

"You want your sister to end up on a farm for the rest of her life?" Ma's voice went sad. "All I want is a good husband for her."

"All Ba wants is the money," Kwok said bitterly.

"You think this is a good life?" Ma asked plaintively. She lowered her voice. "It was me who told your father to ask Dickson home. It was me. Don't blame your father, hear?"

SEVEN

A^T the front of the classroom, Old Abercrombie stood with the textbook to his nose, reading loudly and dramatically from *Romeo and Juliet*. The lines came out in a strong Cambridge accent. Abercrombie's reverence of Shakespeare was evident by the plaster bust of the playwright in the room. It perched on its own fluted pedestal near the front: white, silent and all-seeing.

All morning Kwok had been looking out the window: gazing at the clouds, glancing at the old farmhouse across the way, scanning the sky for birds. Every time he heard Abercrombie turn the page, he did the same. Scribbled history notes lay partly tucked under the Shakespeare. Abercrombie never walked around, never called on him, so Kwok always felt safe in English class. He started checking his memorization: 1837 was Mackenzie's rebellion. Two men had been hanged for treason.

Kwok had thumbed ahead and finished *Romeo and Juliet* long ago. When family tyrants interfered with young love, they could only create suffering and grief. Not that he thought Ying would ever die by her own hand. But he knew things were unfair. All his life he had known that. He was never taken out of school to help plant or harvest. Kwok only had to help with farmwork, while Ying washed dishes, wrung out clothes and heavy bedsheets by hand and pickled barrels of mustard greens — all after doing her share of the farm chores.

But Ma had already made up her mind about the marriage. And Ba wasn't about to do anything. He wouldn't budge about selling to Drysdale, even if it meant not marrying off his daughter to a stranger. He was more concerned about his land.

Kwok had never really given much thought to Ying's future before now. Of course, he had assumed that she would get married some day and have her own life. There were plenty of young men in Chinatown and ample time for love and marriage after high school. All those soccer players, for example, shared more in common with her than Dickson Lee.

A sharp rapping sounded at the door, and Major Gale's head popped in. "Mr. Abercrombie, I need to see you and Philip Scott for a second."

Phil stood up and strode confidently to the door, brushing at his clothes. "Hey, I want no trouble in here while I'm gone," he said to his buddies with a smirk.

Abercrombie fumbled with some vague instructions to the class, and then he and Phil left the room. Kwok went back to his studying, one hand covering the column of notes. During the War of 1812 the Americans had invaded Canada, and then the Canadians had struck back by burning Washington.

Conversations bubbled all around him. Kwok looked down at his notes and tried another date.

Then he heard Taylor's gleeful voice whispering loudly.

". . . so Phil's turning left and then this old farm truck comes ripping through the red light. They barely miss each other and the old truck smacks into a wall. Then his old man comes running out and grabs Phil and starts cursing and shouting, 'You pay me. You makee me crashee, you breakee my truck, you pay me back.' "

Kwok heard giggling and chuckling, and sensed heads turning around to peer at him. He pretended not to hear. Suddenly he hated the school and everyone in it.

Taylor went on. "Of course, Phil says he's not paying, but his old man keeps on screaming and pulling at him. He was probably going to pull out a cleaver and cut Phil up. But then this policeman gets there. And suddenly they're surrounded by all these Chinese laundrymen, out delivering their wash. His old man starts pushing this cop around, can you believe it? Keeps on screaming like a chimpanzee, 'He makee me crashee, he pay me.' "

His audience muttered and shook their heads in disbelief.

"That's not how it happened," Kwok said loudly from the back of the room. Heads whipped up in surprise as the classroom fell silent. He clenched his fists and strode towards Taylor. "You're making things up."

"Oh, yeah?" Taylor's eyes taunted him. "Every-one can see your old truck out there. Still has its busted headlamp. You saying there was no accident?"

"My father doesn't talk like that," Kwok said evenly. "And no policeman or laundrymen came by."

"So?"

"So take it back."

"Ah, beat it." Taylor waved dismissively and turned back to his friends. But Kwok grabbed his collar and hurled him out of his seat like a sack of potatoes. Taylor flew into the blackboard and crashed to the floor. Instantly the entire class leapt to its feet, scrambling and shouting.

Taylor looked momentarily startled, then charged at Kwok with a roar. The two boys shoved and slammed each other against the wall, heaving and twisting. Kwok heard his shirt rip, and then his face smashed into the blackboard ledge and he felt blood spurt from his nose. He threw himself at Taylor, landing several hard punches at his stomach.

Suddenly the Shakespeare bust tipped over and shattered into a million chalky fragments. The two boys were grappling for each other's throats, grunting like wild animals, when Major Gale and Phil tore them apart.

"Kwok-ken Wong!" The principal's glasses hung lopsided from one ear. "Have you lost your mind?"

Phil was dusting the plaster shards off Taylor. Kwok shrugged off the restraining hands and staggered out the door.

"Hey, dummy," Taylor shouted after him. "I didn't make anything up. That's how I heard it from Phil."

***

"Why did you do it, Kwok?" Ying was almost shouting at him. "Even you said Ba behaved like an imbecile."

The Model T sped down the road and the two teens bounced unmercifully on the hard seats over every bump and pit. Kwok had spent the afternoon serving a detention, while Ying waited and waited.

He shook his head. "It was a matter of pride and self-respect, remember?"

"So what was accomplished? Look at your shirt. You might have broken your nose."

He shrugged. "I feel better. I hate those fellows."

"Boys are such fools," she said angrily.

"What about you?" Kwok retorted. "I can't believe you're going along with this scheme to marry Dickson Lee. You could report Ba to Major Gale and say that he's selling you off against your will. He could stop it. Or you could go to the police. Then you could finish school."

"Finish school and then what?" Ying gave him a hard look. "Dickson speaks English, he seems like a nice man. At least he's not sixty years old."

"You don't know him at all. You've met him once."

"Ma knows his family. She's not about to send me off to the jungles with a gorilla, for goodness' sake."

"I can't believe you're talking like this, as if it were a good idea."

"Ba is trying to save the farm, can't you see that? If I can help him, I will."

"But what about you?"

"Me? Who cares about me?" Ying's eyes hardened. "I've got no friends, I never go anywhere. Ba has chores for me, and then Ma has chores for me. The work never ends. If I marry Dickson, things will change. I'll keep my hands clean. Maybe I'll meet people, and there might be dancing and movies for me."

"I wish Ba would sell to Drysdale," Kwok said.

"I wish you'd think things through, you deadhead," Ying said hotly. "Even if Ba sells to Drysdale, do you think my life would turn out any differently? Ma would still marry me off." She paused. "With Dickson, at least I'm useful to Ba."

***

The signs at the gas station in Chinatown offered a tempting range of services: trading of used cars and trucks, grease service, crankcase inspection, lubrication, washing and repairs. The Soon brothers swaggered over with easy smiles. They had done a lot of work on the Model T before and were familiar with the old beast. They looked over the damage and nodded.

"Won't take long," Ernie said. "An hour and a half. You can wait inside the office."

Kwok and Ying went to the truck to fetch their books, but heard a voice calling their names. It was Head Cook, who came running across the road.

"Told myself that truck looks familiar," he said, grinning. "Wah, what happened to your face, Kwok?"

Kwok flinched and twisted away when Head Cook reached out and touched the raw swelling under his eye.

Head Cook backed off. He wore an old blue suit jacket over a collarless shirt, a cap and a pair of brown pants. "Didn't know your truck was getting fixed. How long is the wait?"

"They said an hour and a half."

"Then come and have coffee with me."

The teens hesitated. "We have no money."

"But I do," their friend said cheerfully. "Don't worry, I won big on the soccer game. Paid off all the waiters. Besides, coffee's only three cents a cup. Apple pie, too, best in all of Chinatown at the Hong Kong Cafe. Come along, give a lonely old man like me some company."

Kwok shrugged and Ying nodded. They dumped their books back into the truck and walked out along Main Street. The late afternoon sun warmed them. The street was busy with shoppers and people heading home from work. Head Cook threw one arm over Kwok's shoulder and drew him close. "Why don't you play soccer for Chinatown?"

The older man reeked of tobacco and ketchup, but Kwok couldn't pull away without being rude.

"I don't know these people," he explained patiently. "A team is a team. You have to feel like you fit. I don't belong here."

"Play a bit, then you'd fit," Head Cook advised. "You could make friends here."

Kwok shook his head and tried to pull away. Behind them, Ying looked into the display windows of stores lining the street.

"Chinatown needs you," Head Cook said in a soft voice. "It needs to win the Northwest Trophy. Don't you care about your people?"

"I don't live here."

"You don't have to live in Chinatown to help out."

Kwok shrugged him off and looked away, squinting into the late afternoon sun. A big black Model T honked loudly at a pedestrian, and two girls ran across the street, pushing a wooden hoop along with sticks. When Kwok stopped at the corner to wait for the traffic to clear, Head Cook asked, "Is your father going to sell to Drysdale?"

Kwok was surprised. "How did you find out?"

"Hey, this is Chinatown. We know everything." The older man grinned. "I saw Lee Bing the other day."

"Ba's not selling," Kwok said.

Head Cook nodded approvingly, but then he sighed. "One day, all those farms will vanish."

"So? What difference would it make?"

"Then the city will say, 'The only things the Chinese can do are wash laundry and run restaurants. Who needs them? Let's ship them all back to China.' But everyone needs to eat. They don't think about that. This country needs good farmers."

Kwok shook his head. He couldn't picture it. There were too many Chinese farms along the river. How could they all vanish? It was impossible.

It had been seven or eight years since Kwok had stepped into the Hong Kong Cafe, but little seemed to have changed. At the door, two white men elbowed their way rudely past Head Cook. Kwok felt the fuzzy doormat under his feet, he smelled gravy and coffee, he heard the clink of heavy dishes, and voices speaking the Chinatown dialect rose around him.

Ba had brought him here when he was a little boy. It swelled with noise and laughter then, too, jammed with all kinds of customers, Chinese and white and black. Kwok usually stayed near the door, while Ba drank coffee and joked loudly with friends. Often someone would kneel and push an apple tart into his hand and he would lick the sugar crystals sticking to his fingers for a long time.

The wide glass window of the Hong Kong Cafe gleamed. Behind the long counter were cabinets with sliding glass doors piled high with jelly rolls, doughnuts and cream puffs. A milkshake machine stood poised with shiny metal beaters. Long mirrors lined the room, so everyone could watch all the goings-on. The menu was scrawled in chalk on several blackboards: roast beef, steaks, stew, sandwiches, soups. Rice was the only Chinese food that appeared on the cafe's dishes. Nothing cost more than a quarter.

"Hey, Head Cook!" a friendly voice called out. T.C. waved at them from deep in the back, where he sat at a big table. The Chinese Soccer Team players and friends surrounded him.

Kwok glared angrily at Head Cook. He had stepped into a trap.

"Kwok, good to see you again." T.C. hurried forth, his hand stretched out for a shake. He stopped when he saw Kwok's face. "What happened? You been in a fight?"

Kwok shrugged and T.C. went on. "Come and meet the fellows."

"Uh, I don't think so," said Kwok, turning away. "We've got to go."

But Head Cook was already pushing Ying down towards the back, holding her firmly by the arm. He seemed to know everyone, nodding hellos to those calling at him from the booths or swivelling around from the counter.

T.C. pulled Kwok along. "The team meets here every week. We used to have a coach, but not anymore. People come and tell us what we're doing wrong. The cafe gives us free coffee and apple pie." He grinned. "Sometimes we see more of our team here than at the games because the food's so good."

"Listen, I'm sorry about yesterday," Kwok said nervously.

"Don't worry about it. It's all right if you can't play with us. Everyone has to make up their own mind."

"Well, then I should say congratulations," Kwok said, relieved. "I hear you guys play for the Northwest Trophy in a couple of days."

"Yep, isn't it amazing? Tomorrow we find out who we'll be pitted against."

"So you really don't need me, do you?" Kwok asked.

T.C. shook his head and leaned in close, lowering his voice. "Our last win was a lucky accident, a fluke. Besides, look at that."

He poked his chin at the corner, where a pair of crutches leaned. "Kew Gin took a bad fall and his ankle is swollen."

Eight team members sprawled around the table, dressed in an assortment of sweaters and sports jackets both old and new. Cups and saucers were strewn everywhere. T.C. quickly provided introductions, but Kwok could remember only half of the names. Spoon, a young man with intense dark eyes, guarded the goal. Kew Gun and Kew Gin were brothers from the prominent Yip family who owned Canton Alley in Chinatown. Anna sat snuggled close to her boyfriend Arthur, and on her other side was her girlfriend May. She smiled and beckoned Ying to sit down beside her. Kew Gin had his foot raised on a chair.

More chairs were pulled up. The waitress set down three more cups of coffee and moved away.

"I've never seen such an angry crowd," Anna was saying. "This is the game you missed yesterday, Kwok. The whites were swearing at their own team. It was really scary. I think some of the men were ready to punch out the goalkeeper."

"Wait until you see the crowd that'll come for the Northwest Trophy," warned Kew Gin. "They would rather see us dead than win the cup."

Then the kitchen door swung open and the cook strode out with a hot apple pie held high. A stubbly white beard covered his jaw and travelled up over his head. He slid the pie onto the table with a flourish and a bow.

"Fresh pie," he cried out. "Eat your fill, hear?" He stood back and waggled his chin at Kwok. "Who's this? Never saw him before."

"He's new," T.C. told him. "We're trying to get him to join the team."

"Good, good." The cook nodded earnestly and spoke rapidly. "Times are tough in Chinatown. Men out of work, men starving, men sleeping outside. But when this team wins, everyone can smile. It's food for the soul. Hey, who's your father?"

Kwok hated this question. "Wong Cheung-hoi," he replied reluctantly.

The man in the long apron frowned. "I know that name."

He stooped and peered intently at Kwok. Suddenly everyone around the table seemed to be staring at him. Kwok took a cautious sip of the scalding hot coffee and tried to look nonchalant.

"Aha, I remember now. He's the farmer, isn't he?" the cook cried out. "The one with the big

105

chunk of land by the river. He gives us vegetables all the time."

When Kwok and Ying exchanged puzzled looks, he explained, "Our church organizes chow mein lunches and tea. We invite the whole city for fund-raising. All the food is donated. It's the only way we can make money." He nodded at Ying. "You must be Ah-Hoi's daughter. I didn't know you were so grown-up already. You have some spare time this weekend? We're going downtown to do a tag day to raise funds for the Chinese Air Force. Pretty girls always bring in more donations."

Ying shook her head shyly.

"Ba, leave her alone," Arthur called out. "She doesn't have time."

"Fah, you leave me alone," said the cook indignantly. "Don't need you to tell me what to do." He looked at Kwok again. "Hey, I know your mother, too. Ask well of her for me, eh? Tell her you met Uncle Chuck, Uncle Chuck from Chilliwack. She'll remember. She used to tell me what a smart boy you— "

An ear-splitting crash exploded at the front of the restaurant. The waitresses screamed, dropping plates of food. The kitchen help came running out, shouting. Kwok quickly craned his neck around the booth divider and gasped.

The cafe's big window had been shattered, and glass shards lay everywhere. Broken glass stuck jaggedly around the frame like cracked ice.

The players leapt up and ran out onto the street. Kwok hurried after them, picking his way through the litter of thick glass. Customers sitting near the front of the restaurant had been badly cut. Blood flowed from their faces, necks and hands. People ran back and forth, babbling in a panic.

A heavy wooden crate the size of a seaman's trunk was up-ended against the counter. It had been thrown through the window. Bound with sharp metal strapping, it must have taken at least three strong men to heave it through.

The word "trophy" was crudely daubed onto the box with red paint.

T.C. and Spoon pushed their way back into the cafe, shaking their heads. "They got away. A big truck."

"They backed up onto the sidewalk and threw it through."

"Who?"

"Soccer fans."

EIGHT

T HE morning light was creeping in steadily, but
Kwok drew the pillow over his head. All night
he had tossed fitfully, wincing every time his
bruised face scraped the pillow. He heard Ying stir,
then she was getting out of bed and dressing. He
dozed off. When she came back from washing, she
poked him hard in the ribs.

"Hey, lazy, wake up!"

He rolled away. "Leave me alone."

"It's soccer day at South Hill," she said brightly.
"Time to take another poke at that ball."

When no answer emerged, her voice softened.
"You feeling bad? From the fight yesterday?"

Kwok groaned into his pillow and Ying left. He
just wanted to lie there like a heavy log. He
couldn't bear to see Taylor's ugly face ever again.
Besides, playing soccer would be impossible,
because the whole team would be on Taylor's side,
glaring and sneering at him. Kwok would have to
play three times as hard to get any cooperation.

Why should I have to keep proving myself? he
thought bitterly. In Chinatown, people like Head
Cook and T.C. want me to play; they know I'm
good.

Ma hurried into the room and tugged him
around gently. She brushed the back of her hand

lightly against his forehead. "No fever there," she remarked. "What's the matter with you?"

Kwok let his head loll away. "Headache," he lied. This was something Ma's eyes and hands could never detect. "Dizzy. My stomach hurts."

"You must have caught some wind," Ma said reproachfully. "Didn't I tell you to dress warmly and wear your hat when you drive the truck? And then fighting like animals yesterday. Don't know when you'll learn to take care of yourself."

Yesterday, when Ba had seen Kwok's face and heard the story from Ying, he had grunted, "Didn't I tell you? No one needs friends like those."

Unexpectedly, Ma had retorted, "What friends? You send him to school out here with the whites, there's always going to be fights like this."

As for the Hong Kong Cafe incident, Ba didn't have a word to say, as if he didn't care at all.

Ma came back shortly and pushed a hot water bottle under the bedding at Kwok's feet. He yelped and kicked out. The metal container was hot enough to scorch flesh. Uncapping a small vial of pungent ointment, Ma rubbed it firmly into Kwok's forehead and chest. He felt his skin tingle and twisted away. Ma threw another blanket over him and asked, "You want to eat?"

"I said my stomach hurts!"

"I'll boil potato soup for you later."

All morning Kwok stayed curled in bed. He tried to fall asleep, but anxiety kept twisting his mind awake. His insides were all knotted up. I've wasted two, three years, he thought bitterly. What a fool

I've been, dreaming that I could do everything my way. All that studying and soccer were nothing but a waste of time. Major Gale could never have gotten a scholarship for me. I'd be stuck on this farm forever if Ma hadn't arranged for Ying to get married. He stared at the textbooks and study notes piled beside the bed and wondered if university was the right way to go. Until now, he had assumed it was the only way. But what a price Ying would have to pay.

At lunchtime Ma boiled him some soup with potatoes and black beans. With some food settling his stomach, he was able to doze off a bit.

All afternoon long, Kwok drifted in and out of sleep, but one scene kept recurring in his mind. The broken window at the Hong Kong Cafe formed a deadly hoop of razor-sharp points. Kwok was dressed in his soccer jersey and shorts, sprinting furiously towards the window and then leaping through the jagged hole. The hole wasn't big enough to go through in an upright position, so he had to dive. Over and over he ran at the window, springing forward with his hands leading. Noisy crowds of Chinatown soccer fans waved and cheered him on. But he never landed on the other side.

Kwok floated up reluctantly to wakefulness when he heard Ma banging around in the kitchen. By the gas lamp's glow in the bedroom doorway he could see that evening had come. Ma always came in first from the fields. She cranked the pump for water, opened the stove to load in coal and kindling, and started the fire. Kwok pulled the blankets up around his shoulders. Fiercely he clamped his eyes shut and tried to empty his mind.

Ma appeared at the doorway. "Nothing wrong now, is there? Better get up and eat."

Kwok grunted. His stomach growled. No matter how sick one was, in this household dinner was never served in bed. He swung his feet to the cool linoleum floor and stretched his arms high over his head.

When Ying darted in for clothes to take to the washing room, Kwok quickly asked, "Who won the game?"

She shook her head. "I don't know. It was an away game, remember?"

He waited a second. "Did Coach Carrothers ask you where I was?"

"No."

"Did anyone from the team come to you?"

"No one talked to me."

Kwok fell back onto the bed and propped his arms under his head. His throat dried up and he swallowed painfully. His sister had the right attitude. From now on, the farther away he stayed from soccer, the better it would be.

Ying glanced at him suspiciously. "You don't look sick to me," she said.

"Seeing you makes me feel better," he shouted at her back.

Tomorrow was Saturday. He wouldn't have to go to school. One of the beams in the pigsty needed fixing. The field for the second sowing of spinach had to be prepared. The final flats of seedlings should be planted.

Maybe farming wasn't so bad, he thought. What if the Wong farm became the biggest operation around? What if prices got better? What if they rented out land like Drysdale? Maybe they could make a decent living.

Then the tired faces of Ma and Ying crowded into his head. Ma wasn't about to let him drop out of school. And Ying really didn't want to stay and face the drudgery of the farm, not if she could get away and help Ba keep his land at the same time.

Kwok's eyes blinked open. Ba stood in the doorway, wiping his hands on a towel. "You're better?" he asked.

Kwok nodded, avoiding his father's gaze.

"Tomorrow, we're going fishing," Ba announced.

"What?"

"Dickson wants to go fishing, so he's coming down here. Early tomorrow."

Kwok shook his head. "I won't go."

Ba snapped, "We're all going."

"I'm sick!"

"Your Ma says it's just some wind."

***

Early the next morning, Kwok awakened to a loud thumping. He heard Ba stride to the door and fling it open. Then his father's voice boomed through the pre-dawn. "Wah, so early?"

"But . . . but you said the earlier we started, the better the fishing would be," Dickson stuttered.

"That's so, that's so," Ba reassured him. "We'll be ready in ten minutes. Ying! Kwok! Get up! Hurry!"

"I brought a big tin of rice porridge for breakfast," Dickson called out. "It's still hot."

Kwok pulled himself up and gingerly touched his face. The swelling was going down. Ying lay stiff and still under her blankets.

He caught a glimpse of her face, pale and drawn in the dim light, before she rolled away. Tears glistened on her cheeks.

Kwok's stomach tightened again as he trudged to the outhouse. The morning was cool, and the soft dawn light lent an air of calm to everything. Ying is making the best of a bad situation, he thought miserably.

When Kwok came back, Dickson was sitting at the table in the main room, industriously unwinding the fishing reels. Ba had switched on the gas lamp. The night before he had hauled in the fishing rods and reels, nets and tackle from the barn — all the gear that Ma had wanted him to sell a few years ago after a particularly bad harvest.

"Good morning, Kwok," Dickson called out cheerfully. "Did I wake you up?"

Kwok stared at the visitor's hands. "What are you doing?"

"Your father told me he had plenty of fishing gear but hadn't fished in six or seven years," Dickson replied. His eyes shone brightly behind his spectacles as his hands moved in a blur. "So I reckoned he'd need some new line. Don't want to hook a fish and lose it because the line is all dried and breaks, do we?"

Kwok shook his head groggily and staggered towards the washing room. When he came out, Ying had joined Dickson at the table. Ba sat with them, carefully sharpening the hooks on a long flat stone. Ma was ladling the rice porridge into bowls.

"Look what Dickson brought me," Ying called out.

In a box cut with cleverly shaped slots lay a fountain pen of tortoise shell and gold, a matching inkwell and a thick book with the word "Diary" embossed on it.

Dickson looked anxiously at Ying. "Do you like it?"

She nodded shyly.

"Better than flowers?"

She nodded emphatically. "Oh, yes."

"Better than chocolates?"

Ma interjected gaily, "If it were candy, Kwok would grab it all."

"Yeah, you wanna marry me?" grinned Kwok.

They all burst out laughing, even Ba.

***

By the time they set forth, the skies had brightened considerably but still hung overcast and grey.

"What if it rains?" Dickson asked. His red hunting jacket had a hood, and his gumboots were glossy and shiny from newness. It had rained overnight, and the ground sagged soft and spongy beneath them.

"With rain, that's even better," Ba exclaimed, leading the way like a parade marshal. "The trout, they have good eyes. Cloud and rain make it harder for them to see clearly. They can see the top of the water, and they can see who's standing on the river bank."

Dickson jolted in surprise. "They can?"

"Of course! Why do you think they have eyes?" Ba asked. "To watch grand opera?"

Kwok grinned in spite of himself. Ba had not talked funny like this in a long time.

Ba shouldered the long fishing rods like flag poles. His overalls were newly washed and neatly mended. He reached the edge of the field and looked up and down the river bank. Fishing boats with their dark nets hanging behind them chugged up to the canneries. A log boom wider than a football field had been floated down from the north, and a tugboat pulled it like a giant pancake towards the sawmill. Seagulls rose, cawing long and mournful as they skittered over the water scavenging for food.

"Have to find a good spot," Ba remarked to Dickson.

The newspaperman nodded agreeably as he struggled to match Ba's pace and keep his boots clean.

"The water moves fast," Ba explained, "so the fish get tired. They look for places where the flow slows down a bit. That's why they come to the river's edge. Besides, there's more bugs and things to eat in the shallow water."

They rounded a curve in the dyke where a deep indentation in the long mud wall caught the water and held it.

Ba called out, "Here, let's try this spot." Everyone except Ma clambered to the top of the dyke. The water was grey and deep, flowing to the ocean in strong, steady currents.

Ying helped Dickson tie a cork and hook to his line, and she let him bait it with a small piece of pork rind. Then, with an awkward throw, he cast his line and crouched down gingerly. He turned to Ma, who leaned against the dyke watching the river with keen eyes. "Aren't you fishing?"

Ma shook her head. "I'm afraid of water."

Dickson nodded. "My mother, too."

Ma leaned close to him, "Grandfather died in this river."

The newspaperman glanced over at Ba, who nodded matter-of-factly. "After we were married, we lived in Chinatown. I didn't want to work with my father, so I found a job at the shingle mill. One day he slipped and fell into the river. He couldn't swim."

Dickson nudged Ba. "Then you moved out here?"

Ba nodded. "I inherited my father's share of the partnership. He always wanted to own his own land; he wanted me to help him. But I was sick of working in the fields in China, so I stayed away. Until I found out how Chinatown had been cheating me all those years. What a fool I was. My father had been right all along. A man's land is the only thing he can rely on. So I borrowed money and bought out the partners."

"We all left Chinatown and moved out here," Ma added. "The first years were so hard. No women around, no children around, no stores, no friends. But Ah-Hoi tried to make the children happy."

Oh, don't make it sound like such a fairy tale, Kwok lashed out silently. Ba didn't rush out here like a noble prince to save his father's land.

"When they were small, I used to bring them out here to fish." Ba cast his line with a smooth, rolling pitch. Then his wrist rotated slowly, flicking the fishing rod gently. "Their mother made me loop a rope around their waists and tie it around myself. I felt like a nursemaid."

"Did anyone fall in?" asked Dickson.

"Yeah, Ba did!" Ying said, laughing.

"Not so," protested her father. "I hit a slippery spot and slid a bit, that's all. Didn't even get wet."

Kwok stuck bait onto his hook. The piece was too large to fool any fish, but he didn't bother trimming it down. Be honest, he thought. We didn't go fishing that many times. Back then, Ba used to gamble and drink every weekend. He and Ma would scream at each other — about money, about the children, about the farmwork. Neither of them wanted to be out here, working the soil. Then Ba got very sick. Kwok remembered Ma sobbing in the dark, her weeping the only sounds all night long. After that, Ba stopped going to Chinatown and settled down.

Kwok jerked his line back and forth erratically, not caring if he caught anything or not.

Dickson was chatting with Ma. "So are you happier now?"

Who could be happy here? thought Kwok. Ma could die from working so hard and Ying is escaping by being married off. Ba wasn't always keen about farming. He preferred gambling. He worked in a mill. Can't he see that I don't want to be here, either? Ba didn't do what his father wanted, but he expects me to.

"Wah, got something!" Ba leapt to his feet and braced himself. His line went taut and the cork was dragged underwater. As Ba started reeling in, the line cut swift, darting curves on the surface of the river.

Dickson's eyes widened with envy and awe when Ba dangled an eight-pound trout in front of them. Pearly grey and glistening, the fish flicked its tail desperately. Ba jumped off the dyke and went to Ma, who had spread newspapers on the ground. With a sharp knife he quickly gutted his catch. Ma blotted the fish dry and placed it gently in the wicker basket she had brought along.

"So fast," Dickson said to Ba, marvelling at his efficiency. "One minute you catch it and the next you've cleaned it."

"You have to be fast or you spoil the taste of the fish." Ba looked pleased with himself. He looked around and grinned cockily. "I'm going to try another spot. If I stay here, you young people won't catch anything."

He strode off, followed by Ma.

"Say, did you hear about the soccer team and the window at the Hong Kong Cafe?" Dickson asked.

"We were there," Ying said.

"Have the police caught anyone?" asked Kwok.

"Are you kidding?" said Dickson. "The police want to see the Chinese Soccer Team scared away, too. No one wants us to win the Northwest Cup." He looked closely at the two teens. "What were you two doing at the cafe?"

"They asked Kwok to join the team," Ying replied.

"Will you?"

Kwok did not answer, and when Dickson looked at Ying, she shrugged.

"The other semi-final match was yesterday," Dickson told him. "The Chinese will be playing Bastion Cigarettes for the trophy."

Kwok's heart started pounding, and his jaw tightened.

"They're a tough team," Dickson continued. "They're big, they're fast, and they play rough. The old-timers in Chinatown don't think we can beat them." He nudged Ying with his elbow. "Will you come watch the game?"

Ying was surprised. "Me?"

"Your whole family, silly." Dickson replied. "Every Chinese in town will be there. It's the biggest event of the decade."

Ying sounded uncertain. "When is it?"

"Tomorrow."

"I don't know," she said hesitantly. "We already took a holiday today. Besides, Ba doesn't like soccer."

"No harm in asking," Dickson said cheerfully.

"Halloo, Mr. Wong!" A voice hailed them from a distance. Back at the farmhouse, a car had driven into the clearing. A tall man in a suit and overcoat waved frantically at them. Kwok peered across the fields, trying to identify the visitor.

"Who is it?" Dickson asked curiously.

Ying shrugged.

"Should we head in?"

They looked downriver where Ba and Ma were fishing. Ma waved energetically at the visitor, but up atop the dyke, Ba had turned his back to the farm and seemed intent on reeling in another trout.

The man in the suit had located the path leading out to the dykes and now strode carefully over the soft mud, trying to avoid the puddles that were everywhere.

As Dickson, Kwok and Ying reached Ba and Ma, Dickson asked, "Who would come all this way?"

Ma shook her head and Ba stared fixedly at the river. All his good humour seemed to have vanished.

The visitor came up, panting slightly. "Mr. Wong?" he asked, not sure who he should address.

Dickson tilted his head at Ba, and the visitor reached up with one hand, offering it for a handshake. "Mr. Wong, I'm James Stone, Everett Drysdale's lawyer."

Ba did not move as the visitor went on. "Mr. Drysdale asked me to come and place another offer before you for your land. Mr. Drysdale has decided, exceedingly generously, if you ask me, to increase his offer to twelve hundred dollars. In cash."

The lawyer's words hung on the river wind. He looked up at Ba, who still had not acknowledged him. "Mr. Wong, did you understand me?"

Ba let out a long breath very slowly, as if he were thinking great thoughts. "Tell Mr. Drysdale my land is not for sale."

"The offer is good for four days," the lawyer said. "Think about it. You won't get another chance." Then he turned and marched away, just as the rain started to fall in large heavy drops.

Kwok kicked angrily at a clod of dirt. The land was more important than anything else to Ba, and not even Ma would be able to change his mind. Ba already resented how Ma had worked against him all these years, planning and plotting to send Kwok away to university.

Kwok leaned against the dyke, staring at the thick grey clouds sweeping in from the ocean. Ba and Ma controlled his life the same way that the weather determined the fate of the farm. Now there was only one thing he could do on his own.

NINE

K WOK crashed through the bushes and puddles along the narrow pathway through the woods. His canvas bag bounced easily on his back now that it carried just soccer gear instead of books. He hoped Ba wouldn't notice his absence too soon. Not that Kwok was too worried. What could his father do, chase him into Chinatown, grab him by the collar and drag him back, kicking and screaming?

After the fishing expedition, when Dickson had invited Ba to the game, Kwok had momentarily hoped that Ba would consent to go. Imagine Ba's mouth dropping open in surprise when Kwok ran onto the field playing for the championship Chinese Soccer Team. But that would give him nowhere near the mountain of satisfaction he would get helping defeat the team from Bastion Cigarettes. He'd make that worm of a driver who had dismissed him sorry.

He glanced at the skies. After a night of steady rain, the heavens still loomed like unyielding grey mountains. Yesterday's downpour had not stopped the fishing, though. After Drysdale's lawyer drove away, Dickson pulled his hood over his head and leaned resolutely against the dyke, holding his fishing rod out like a prayer, even as the black clouds rolled in from the ocean and the rain fell more and more heavily. Ying held an open umbrella over both of them. Ma forced Kwok to head in first to study.

Inside the house, Kwok pretended to read his books, but his mind darted in a million directions as he tried to figure out a way to get to the game. He spent the afternoon fixing the pigsty and tinkering in the barn. Then he sauntered over to Lee Bing's farm.

The old man sat sprawled on his porch, smoking his pipe, sipping a steaming mug of tea and watching the rain come down. The pigs were doing fine, he told Kwok, and the lumber for the new pen had arrived. Then Kwok learned that Lee Bing was indeed driving into town for the championship soccer game.

"Of course I'm going," the old man said indignantly. "I want to see us beat them at their own game."

Now as he approached the neighbouring farm, Kwok could hear that Lee Bing had already cranked up the old truck. He sprinted into the clearing and saw him tucked into the truck, drumming his hands impatiently on the steering wheel.

"Hurry, boy," he called out. Kwok threw his bag on and jumped aboard. Lee Bing's dark blue suit shone with age, and his tie was stained and wrinkled. A felt hat lay on the seat between them.

Kwok held his breath until the truck had chugged up over the hill and began coasting smoothly into mid-town. Every time Lee Bing shifted gears, clinking sounds ground through the engine.

Lee Bing chewed nonchalantly on tobacco. Suddenly he shouted over the noise, "What did the man in the fancy car want yesterday?"

Kwok hated nosy neighbours. "Which man?"

"The big tall one, stupid boy. Who else?"

"Oh, that one. Everett Drysdale's lawyer."

"So will your Ba sell?" Lee Bing demanded.

Kwok shook his head. "The lawyer offered him twelve hundred dollars, but Ba still said no."

"Good for him!" exclaimed Lee Bing, slapping the steering wheel with glee. "Good news indeed."

A streak of irritation flared in Kwok. "If he sold, Ma could live in a new house."

Lee Bing sighed. He stared fixedly at the road. "Drysdale wants to evict all the farmers along River Road. That's thirty, forty farms. Then he could lay out his golf course in no time. Only your father can keep us all from ending up at the soup kitchen. He owns land right in the middle."

Kwok gritted his teeth. My father the great hero, he thought sarcastically. Wants to help everyone except his own family. All the farmers will crowd around and shake his hand, but they don't care one bit about Ying or me.

They drove the rest of the way without saying another word. Kwok looked out his window, clenching and unclenching his hands anxiously. Would the Chinese Soccer Team let him play? What if they did and he played with two left feet?

As they drew closer to the playing ground, traffic on the road and sidewalks thickened. People of all ages streamed towards the match: families with grandparents and babies, gangs of teenagers, young couples. It reminded Kwok of summer exhibition time, when everyone flocked to the fairgrounds for the circus, horse races and midway games.

Today people tugged folding chairs, wooden stools and even stepladders along with their umbrellas and raincoats. Lee Bing's truck fell behind a long line of tooting, stalled automobiles. Cursing, Kwok hopped out of the truck and started running, dodging and weaving his way through the crowds. Good way to warm up, he thought.

At the corner of the field, enterprising souls bustled behind makeshift stoves. "Hot dogs and soda pop, right here!" they called. "Popcorn, peanuts and floss!"

The salty-sweet aromas of sausages and caramel set hunger pangs drumming inside Kwok, but he had neither time nor money. He raced by the vendors and almost knocked down two thin Chinese standing nearby. They carried cardboard signs and jangled coin-filled boxes with slots on them. Kwok couldn't read the Chinese words scrawled on the sign, but guessed they were part of the war relief fundraising.

The rickety wooden bleachers had already been filled by the early arrivals. The crowd by the sideline stood ten, fifteen deep, held back from the turf and the team enclosures by taut ropes. The whites had gathered on one side, and the Chinese were on the other. A dozen burly policemen patrolled the field.

Kwok ran through the crowds and past the bleachers. Nearing midfield, he saw the team area guarded by league officials wearing red armbands. They shooed away newspaper photographers and curious fans alike.

"Kwok!" T.C. waved to him and quickly pulled him inside the ring of guards. The players he had met at the Hong Kong Cafe gathered around him. A few smiled, the rest seemed restless and anxious. They looked cold and small in their royal blue shorts and jerseys, with coats draped over their shoulders. Kwok looked from face to face for a flicker of welcome.

Hesitating, he asked, "Do you have enough players? I thought . . . if you needed someone . . . or if you were shorthanded . . . maybe I could help out . . . if you still wanted . . . "

Eddie crossed his arms over his chest.

"We don't need latecomers," he barked out. "You can't waltz in at the last minute and expect to play."

Kwok deflated. Eddie was right. There was no place for him here. He had been crazy to come.

Arthur spoke up. "But we asked him to join, remember?"

Kwok squirmed, dismayed to be the centre of attention. "I just want to help," he blurted.

"You want to be a big shot hero?"

"No!" Kwok shook his head adamantly. He couldn't say he was here for his own personal revenge against Bastion. Instead, he took a deep breath and said, "After they threw that wooden trophy through the window, I wanted you to get the real thing. Then maybe you can throw it back through the window of city hall."

T.C. looked at him sadly. "We've got just enough players to start with. Everyone wants to play. This is the biggest game of the season. I can't drop anyone now."

***

The coin toss sprung the ball to Bastion, so when the whistle tooted, a redhead whipped the ball away. It dropped to midfield, where Bastion flicked it around casually to see how the ball took to the mucky ground. Then they attacked with a series of short, savage passes.

The Chinese shadowed closely. T.C. ran after the centre with the bushy moustache, but the ball went away, high. Landing far to the side, it spun like a downhill shotput. Eddie and Redhead tore after it together. Eddie inched ahead, but just as he touched the ball, a sudden shove from Redhead sent him stumbling.

Foul! shouted Kwok from the sidelines, expecting play to stop, expecting the Chinese to get the ball. But no whistle sounded. The Chinese fans booed furiously.

Kwok craned his neck and looked around. Where was the referee? Hadn't he seen? Redhead had scooted into centre field. Eddie ran after him, fury propelling him. Redhead flicked the ball away just as he arrived, and Kwok could see the two players exchange angry words.

The ball moved swiftly across the field several times. A burly player from Bastion took the ball after a series of fast, hard punts and shot at the Chinese net. Spoon the goalkeeper scooped it and fed it deftly to Kew Gun, running through from behind. Instantly, Burly pounced on him. Kew Gun dodged him like a dancer. But then his foot twisted in the mud. Cursing, he drove the ball backwards. The pass veered wide and Redhead intercepted and booted it to centre, where a gaping hole suddenly yawned. Kwok groaned as Moustache dashed out of nowhere and fired the ball high into the net.

The Chinese fans fell deathly silent, but the other half of the crowd unleashed a gigantic cheer, filling the air with whistles and hoots.

Kwok cursed angrily and watched as T.C. ran from player to player, reassuring them. When the ball came back into play, the Chinese were hammered without mercy. Bastion players appeared everywhere, they moved fast, and all their passes connected. The action moved back and forth as the two teams rushed at each other. Every time the Chinese team drew near the Bastion goal, an eager swell of anticipation bubbled among the Chinese fans. Kwok had never seen the Bastion team in action before, and he marvelled grudgingly at how they seemed to have no weak spots at all.

What didn't make sense was the rough play. Bastion's natural strength gave them every chance of winning this game. So why did they have to play like drunken bullies?

Redhead broke away and charged the Chinese goal. Arthur rushed him. Redhead feinted and kicked, but his boot flew over the ball and smashed into Arthur's shin. Arthur howled and fell to the mud, clutching his leg in agony. When the referee shouted, "Play on, play on!" the Chinese fans rose in a giant wave, booing and hissing. Arthur limped around for a while before he could put full weight on his leg. And then the play resumed.

Kwok shook his head. The other league games he had watched with the Chinese team hadn't been like this. But this was a championship match between whites and Chinese. Bastion wanted the trophy and knew they could get away with playing dirty. And there was nothing the Chinese could do.

Minutes later, the whistle signalled half-time. The teams parted to the sidelines with the score at 1-0. Arthur crashed to the ground like a beached whale, panting in agony, oblivious to the mud oozing under him. The others walked tight circles and bent over to catch their breath.

T.C. and the team manager knelt by Arthur, gingerly inspecting his injury. Then T.C. looked over at Kwok and called out, "Get your boots on. Arthur isn't going to play anymore."

Kwok pulled off his sweaters and laced his boots. Suddenly he wasn't sure he wanted to play. The Bastion team was ruthless and racist, and the referee wasn't doing anything to stop them. Playing good soccer seemed irrelevant here.

"What the hell is going on?" Head Cook burst into the ring lugging two heavy kettles and enamel mugs. The team tightened around him for lukewarm tea. "That referee, he must be tired of his life!"

The players took mugs and retreated, slurping loudly, too winded to talk.

"There'll be a riot if he doesn't watch out!" Head Cook shouted, banging the mugs around like a street vendor. "Does he think we're all blind?"

"There's a dozen policemen out there to protect him," T.C. said coldly. "Do you think he's worried?"

The team swigged their tea and spat onto the ground. Kwok looked around cautiously. No one came to talk to him until Head Cook arrived with a mug. He nodded approvingly. "You did right, coming out to play."

Kwok grunted. "Haven't played yet."

Head Cook pointed at the stands full of Bastion supporters. "They think the Chinese don't know anything," he muttered. "But we've got eyes, we know what's right!"

Applause burst in the bleachers on the other side as Bastion started sending players back onto the field. The Chinese took final gulps of tea and tossed their mugs back. As they headed out, the Chinese fans started clapping in unison.

T.C. darted up to Kwok. "You play centre," he said. "I'm taking Arthur's spot."

"But I'm new," Kwok protested.

"Exactly. A new face will throw them off. They don't know how you play."

***

"Hey, Chinaman, you play soccer? I hear in China the balls have corners on them!"

Kwok glanced at Redhead on the centre line and looked away. Freckles and a nose big as a lightbulb. His eyes glared like a guard dog's. Kwok tried to stare through him. Don't think about him, he told himself. Just watch the ball.

"Hey, Chinaman, what's the matter? You no speakee English?"

Then the whistle sounded and Kwok quickly put the ball into play. T.C. broke free and streaked down left field. Two Bastion men tailed him. Kwok and Eddie sprinted down the centre, waiting for him. T.C. was an arm ahead of his nearest pursuer, who suddenly tackled. The foot aimed for the ball, but it tripped T.C. instead. T.C. went sprawling into the mud.

"Foul!" shouted Kwok. "Foul!"

The referee wasn't looking. Or listening. Kwok started towards him, but Eddie grabbed him.

"Leave it," he muttered, pushing him back.

"It's not fair."

"Forget it." Eddie twisted Kwok's collar tight and forced him to meet his eyes. "Who said things were fair? This is the way things are. Understand?"

Kwok swallowed hard. So this was what it was like to play for a Chinese team. The Bastion fans were clapping and shouting in unison. Someone was leading them in a group cheer. Two beats of hand claps were followed by calls of "Win! Win!" Two claps followed, and then the call was "Kill! Kill!" Over and over they thumped out the challenge, and Kwok had to shake his head to block out the sound.

Kwok and T.C. didn't touch the ball much during the next quarter. Kee went behind the defenders to cover any breaks. The midfielders and Ernie played deep, too, to fortify the defence. Kwok and T.C. stayed upfield as strikers and kept their markers busy.

From afar, Kwok saw that the thickened defence was slowing Bastion. Their passing was still accurate, especially the knee-high crosses and low chip shots. But now the Chinese were intercepting more and more. Bastion jumped and charged and pushed them at every chance. Then Kai limped off the field, his ankle swollen like a balloon after a vicious tackle from Bastion, and the team manager came in nervously as a replacement. Kwok could feel the disappointment and worry swirling in the stands.

A few minutes later, the referee nailed a foul against Bastion. Finally! Kwok could hardly believe it. He licked his lips, tasting the salt of his sweat. Moustache had tripped Kee twenty feet from Bastion's penalty line.

Six Bastion players linked arms and formed a wall in front of the goal. They taunted the Chinese with obscene gestures and lewd insults. "Hey, sucker! No one crosses the Great White Wall!"

T.C. set the ball on the penalty spot, far left of the goal. He stood back to ponder his shot.

"Come on, sissy boy! Show us something!" Bastion taunted.

"Whoo! Whoo!"

Then Eddie darted up and across the wall. He dropped into the end slot like an extra man for Bastion and blocked the goalkeeper's view for a moment. The goalie hopped up to watch T.C., but in the next second, Kee tore up at an angle and fired the ball over the wall and into the net!

Ho-hoo! The cheering from the Chinese erupted like a clap of thunder. A thick forest of arms and scarves, newspapers and umbrellas billowed in the stands, exultant.

The score was tied. Bastion whirled back like a tornado, but now their attack began to dissolve. Without their one-point lead, they seemed panicky. Their passes went askew, they fired at the net from too far out. When they lost the ball, the Chinese moved it into centre field, but there it stayed.

Then Kwok took a long pass from Ernie and headed for the Bastion goal. Two men came at him in midfield. Kwok met Thick Lips head on, then faked him to one side before pivoting and running past him.

When Moustache moved in, Kwok spun around and headed back home. Then he centred the ball to Ernie, who raced for the goal through a sudden hole. All of Bastion converged on him. He reached the net, ready to fire. But at the last minute, Ernie chipped the ball to his right, where T.C. suddenly appeared. And he blasted the ball in high over the goalkeeper!

The crowd on the Chinese side of the bleachers screamed long and loud like a blast of pent-up steam. Again Kwok forced himself to concentrate. The last thing they needed was to go into overtime.

Slow minutes later, the final whistle sounded and the fans from Chinatown leapt onto the field. The Chinese players danced into one another, arms high, whooping and shouting like children. Before Kwok could move, the crowd swallowed them. He tried pushing his way out, shoving aside the hands reaching to shake his, ducking the arms clapping his shoulders. All around, people laughed and cheered. Kwok gasped for air. Taking a deep breath, he threw himself outside the scrum of flailing bodies.

Someone touched his shoulder gently. It was Head Cook, smiling softly. "Your father, he doesn't understand Chinatown, but it's good that you do."

From behind the bleachers, huge triangular flags of green, yellow and pink unfurled. Flung out like the sails of an ocean schooner, they bore the names of Chinatown clubs. The hubbub on the field grew wilder and louder. Grown men chanted together like drunken teenagers, women threw their heads back, giggling giddily, and children ran everywhere. No one cared how deep their feet sank into the soft mud.

"We won!" Kwok shouted. "We did it!"

A young woman smiled enormously and screamed, "Congratulations!"

He opened his arms and she hugged him tight. Then the piercing blare of a trumpet jolted them. They looked away, and there on the street a marching band in braided uniforms and tassled caps waved shiny brass horns and rattled their drums. A cacophony of automobile horns called out and the crowd swept off the field in one big tide.

At the sidewalk, T.C. and the team manager posed for newspaper photographs. Between them, they held up the Northwest Trophy, a gleaming silver cup three feet high and a foot around. Behind them, the team pushed and mugged their way into camera range.

A reporter was firing questions at T.C. when the two war canvassers, still wearing their cardboard signs, suddenly pushed in and ripped open their boxes. With a dramatic flourish, they poured a stream of coins into the gigantic trophy cup. The crowd cheered.

"For war relief!" shouted T.C. He shook the cup and the cash jingled.

Then people all around started pulling out purses and wallets and throwing money into the trophy. Pennies, nickels, dimes, quarters and even bills flew forward. The camera flashed again. T.C. thrust the cup at the reporter, who was forced to drop some coins in before the crowd applauded him.

T.C. and Kee clambered onto the back of a waiting truck. They waved for Kwok. "Come on!" A tangle of eager hands reached out and pulled Kwok safely aboard. T.C. threw an arm around him and waved happily at the crowd milling below them.

"Isn't this great?" he shouted.

A thundering drumroll launched the parade. The five huge flags went first, flapping gloriously in the wind. Then came the marching band. Next were the three trucks full of beaming soccer players. Their fans filled the road, halting the oncoming traffic. Angry drivers honked impatiently, adding to the noise travelling to Chinatown. On the sidewalks, watching with eyes both bemused and resentful, were the other citizens of Vancouver.

"We're making a traffic jam," Kwok shouted at Eddie.

"Who cares?" Eddie hollered back. "Chinatown hasn't ever been this happy!"

The parade sailed through a red light, stopping more traffic. People ran alongside the trucks to shake hands with the team. Dickson Lee ran up and thrust bottles of soda pop into their hands.

"Well done, Kwok-ken!" he shouted, pumping Kwok's hands vigorously. Kwok found himself smiling at everyone.

"You're number one!"

"We played their game and showed them who's the best!"

As the parade rolled into Chinatown, long strings of firecrackers, hanging from every balcony, exploded and shook the air like gunfire. The trucks stopped at the Peking Restaurant and the crowds pressed in.

"Come on." Eddie pulled at Kwok as people jostled at the restaurant door. "There's free food for everyone!"

"Everyone?"

"Yep! All Chinatown's been invited!"

If only this day could last forever, Kwok exulted. He couldn't believe how perfectly it had turned out.

Then he felt someone else tug hard at his arm. When he turned, he saw Ying, her face wet and dark. Mud covered her overalls and rubber galoshes, and her hands hung red and raw.

"Kwok, the river broke through the dykes," she cried out. "The asparagus field was flooded away. We've lost it."

TEN

Wᴵᵀᴴ his mind reeling, Kwok followed Ying as she ran through the crowds to the Wongs' truck. He bent over and cranked the starter furiously, praying for it to cooperate. When it coughed to life, they jumped in and drove off as if lives were at stake.

Ying caught her breath and started to explain. "This morning, Ba and I were planting lettuce when all of a sudden Ma came running over, screaming and waving her bandanna. She kept shouting, 'We're all dead! We're all dead!' She was crying and choking, all bent over from shouting and running. I've never seen her like that. Ba and I raced over to the asparagus field and it was as if it had never been there. All you could see was the water. The current collapsed the dykes on the upriver side and swept everything away."

"And the rest of our fields?"

"The other dykes are holding up. For now, anyways."

Kwok blasted his horn at a slow-moving driver and tried to quell the waves of panic and guilt rising in him. Hotly, he demanded, "Didn't you do anything?"

"Of course we did," Ying said indignantly. "First we looked all over for you. Then we drove over to Lee Bing's place and dragged away the planks he had bought for his pig pen. We waded out into the river and tried to use them to block the water. But it didn't work. Then we went to get sandbags. But the gravel yard was closed and the quarry pit said they needed money up front. That's their new policy. Thirty percent down."

"Special deal for Chinese farmers, right?" Kwok's face was grim.

The Model T roared through an intersection, forcing a pedestrian to leap back. "Slow down!" Ying shouted. "Do you want to kill someone?"

Then she went on. "When we went home, Ma was at the edge of the field, tears streaming down her face. We all just stood there, staring at the field. And then Ba told me to go to town and tell Drysdale he was ready to sell."

"What?" Kwok's mind floundered.

Ying shrugged. "Mr. Drysdale said he'd come over this afternoon with the documents. I saw him before I went to look for you."

Kwok shook his head, not able to believe Ying's words.

"Ba's given up," she said. "But you should be happy. Things are turning out just the way you want."

"You can finish high school," Kwok said weakly. "And say good-bye to Dickson."

The traffic light at King Edward Avenue seemed stuck on red. Kwok lowered his head and glared at it like a sprinter. "Come on, come on," he muttered.

His hands gripped the steering wheel so tightly that his knuckles were white.

When the light changed, the truck jolted forward with a lurch. Kwok's eyes were locked on the road rushing at him, but his mind was spinning.

Ba was going to sell. Now that it was about to happen, Kwok found it impossible to think of a green golf course replacing their farm. It wasn't what he had expected to feel.

"Ba can't sell," he said finally. "If he does, Drysdale will evict all the farmers."

"What?" Ying turned to him, alarmed. "What are you saying, Kwok?"

Kwok's voice was low and urgent. "If Ba sells, that means all the farms will vanish. Soon no one will know there were ever Chinese farmers."

"What do you care?" Ying demanded. "You're going away to university."

"No I'm not."

"But all your life — "

"I never saw people treat the Chinese so badly as today," Kwok interrupted. "The white soccer fans wanted to wipe the grass with our blood. The refereeing stank worse than pig manure. Then we won, and for the first time in my life I felt I belonged somewhere. It was a brand new feeling for me. It felt good, to be able to help Chinatown. And farms are a part of that community."

"But what about Ma?" Ying persisted.

"If I stay and work the farm full time," Kwok said slowly, "then she can do less."

Ying shook her head. "I wasn't talking about the farm. What will Ma say when she hears you're not going to university?"

***

The Model T pulled into the clearing. Kwok jumped out and ran towards the asparagus field. When he got there, he stopped in his tracks. Ying was right. The field with its orderly rows of green plants had completely disappeared under the murky grey river. Kwok could see now how much lower the asparagus had been situated. The only way they could reclaim the field would be to drop sandbags into the water and build a wall out into the river, one foot at a time. And then they would have to drain the water slowly off the submerged land, either with a water wheel or a pump. Even then, the plants would be dead and they would have to start from seed all over again.

Ba squatted on the ground, looking darkly over his loss. His overalls were soaking wet. Kwok came up slowly. His father's eyes were fixed blankly on the river where his field had once been.

"Ba," he called out, "don't sell the land to Drysdale."

His father didn't look at him.

Kwok started hesitantly. "Ba, I know I shouldn't have gone to play soccer, but the team asked me to help."

Ba let out a long breath. "If they asked you jump off a tall building, would you jump?"

Kwok shrugged. "Ba, don't sell the land to Drysdale."

"Don't speak nonsense, stupid boy."

"I want to farm," Kwok said loudly. "Really. I want to work on this farm."

"You hate farmwork," countered Ba bluntly. "For the past three years, you've been planning for university. You want to leave here and never come back."

"Don't sell," Kwok begged. "You wouldn't sell when the lawyer came down here the other day."

"I changed my mind."

"So did I."

"Look at this." Ba gestured broadly over the water. "Two years of work. All gone. In ten seconds, the field turns into water." Ba shook his head. "I can fight Drysdale and Taro Head, but not the river."

"I can help you," Kwok offered. "I don't want to go to university."

Ba didn't seem to have heard him. "I borrowed money to buy this land. I thought land could never be taken away from you. I thought land would last forever. Now it is gone."

"We'll start the asparagus again next year in the lettuce field. This field can wait. In two or three years, things will get better. We can build new dykes then."

Ba turned to look at his son. "Your mother wants you to go to university."

Kwok glanced back at the farmhouse, where Ying and Ma were standing. If he could convince

Ba to wait to fix the dykes, maybe Ying would at least have a choice about marrying Dickson. Even from far away, he could see the dejected stoop in Ma's shoulders. But there was no turning back now. He would have to deal with her anger and disappointment later. "Does Ma want all the farms to disappear?" Kwok asked his father. "Fifty, sixty years of history. It will be as if we never existed. As if Chinese don't do anything but wash laundry and open restaurants."

Ba looked at him suspiciously. "Where did you learn to talk like that?"

"Nowhere."

"Fah!"

"Chinatown, then."

"There are fools in Chinatown, just as there are on these farms."

Ba fell silent and they watched a gigantic log coast by, bouncing in the rapid waters like a twig. Then Kwok asked quietly, "Was my grandfather a fool?"

An impatient toot of an automobile horn broke into their thoughts. Ba and Kwok glanced at each other and headed back in.

Drysdale leaned against his automobile, one foot high on the running board, one hand playing with the cigar jutting from his mouth. A man clutching a big camera waited behind him. Ma and Ying stood anxiously on the porch.

"Good afternoon!" Drysdale called out jovially. "I came as soon as Mr. Stone prepared the legal papers." Then he introduced the photographer. "I wanted some pictures to mark this day. This is the start of my biggest project."

He reached inside his jacket and pulled out a sheaf of papers. He dabbed his forehead with a handkerchief. "Here," he said, thrusting the documents at Ba. "Sign on the last page." Then he pulled out another long cigar and handed it gallantly to Ba. He struck a match and Ba bent to put his cigar into the light cupped by Drysdale's palm. When he straightened up, a small flame flicked at the tip of the cigar. But instead of blowing it out, Ba tipped one corner of the papers into the flame. The papers ignited immediately.

Drysdale grabbed for them. "Are you crazy? Stone spent hours preparing those."

But Ba held the burning papers high like a torch. A thin trail of dark smoke soared skywards.

"You fool!" Drysdale screamed. "Do you know what you're doing?"

The papers crackled, and brown cinders fled into the wind.

Ba nodded slowly. "I know," he said.

Behind the flames that Ba held came late rays of sunshine. When Ba turned from Drysdale, his dark face sprang into light. Kwok saw the wrinkles and lines carved into his father's face like a pattern of roots. Then a shy old smile tugged at Ba's lips. Kwok grinned, and let out a long breath of relief. With the warmth of the sun bathing him, he walked over to his father.